To Love a Warrior

The Isle of Mull Series, Volume 3

Lily Baldwin

Published by Lily Baldwin, 2014.

To Love a Warrior is a work of fiction. Names, characters, places, and incidents are the product of the author's imagination or are used fictitiously. Any resemblance to actual events, locales, or persons, living or dead, is entirely coincidental.

This book is dedicated to Dan. Your support and love mean everything to me.

Thank you to my beautiful and loving mom and to the fabulous Kathryn Lynn Davis. This book never would have happened without your care and assistance. Thank you to all of the readers who have accompanied me on this journey. And to Susan ~ I love you.

Chapter One
Prologue
Isle of Mull, Scotland
Winter 1294

A deafening clap of thunder rebounded off the stones of Dun Ara Castle pulling Shoney from her slumber. Then a white light flashed before her eyes, warning her that a vision was forthcoming.

She saw a cloaked figure, holding fast to a small bundle, shielding it from the fierce storm, which pounded the moors with stinging rain and blazed the night sky with white lightning. Still, the figure pushed onward. Then the rain ceased, and blackness fell but only for a moment. The clouds parted, and a full moon revealed the figure standing amid moss-covered stones at the foot of a hill. But the bundle was gone.

When her vision dissipated, Shoney cast aside her cover, and in one fluid movement, she rose from the bed, leaving its warmth and Ronan behind. She yanked the brown folds of her tunic over her long, silver hair and settled it over her linen shift. Not bothering to belt her waist, she put on her leather slippers and grabbed her thickest cloak. Then, with neither hesitation nor fear, she stepped out into the night and into the storm.

Trudging inland to the open moors, she looked to the heavens just as a bolt of lightning spread its luminous fingers across the sky, revealing bleak, wintry hills that stretched out endlessly before her, but only for an instant; then the light was gone, replaced once more with murky darkness. She was soaked through to the skin, her body stooped from the weight of her water-logged cloak and tunic, but she was not deterred. Something powerful had beckoned her, needed her—and she would answer its call.

There were only two things she knew for certain. First, she had to make haste to the hill she had glimpsed in her vision, and second, whatever it was that waited for her there would unequivocally change her life.

At last, Shoney arrived at the base of the hill. She moved along the stones, certain they held a treasure that was meant for her. Hidden among the tallest of the rocks, she spotted the tiny bundle the cloaked figure in her vision had been carrying. She bent low and folded back a piece of sodden wool, exposing the face of a sweet babe. It was tiny and icy cold to the touch. Even with the wind howling, Shoney could hear the baby's raspy breaths.

Wasting no time, she scooped the infant into her arms, wrapping the folds of her cloak tightly around them both. But before she began their journey home, Shoney crooned, "Everything is just as it should be." Then she dipped her head, placing a kiss on the baby's brow. When her lips touched the infant's forehead a white light flashed in Shoney's mind. She prepared herself for yet another vision.

The badge of the Mackinnon, a Scottish pine branch, was suspended high against the starry sky. There was a stillness in the air and an eerie silence, which was broken suddenly as the branch burst into bright flames, and in the distance, Shoney heard a single warrior sound the battle cry of the MacKinnon.

Shoney snapped back to full awareness. She did not understand the significance of her vision but divining the truth would have to wait until both she and the babe were warm and dry. As if to hasten her onward, the storm intensified. Lightning cut once more through the clouds and thunder shook the ground, creating a din like that of an army on the move.

As silent as she could, Shoney entered the great hall and sat with the child by the fire. She wrapped the babe in a clean plaid, then cradled her close and fed her some goat's milk.

"Ye will be called Nellore," Shoney told her as she drank hungrily, "feral one."

At dawn, Shoney awoke still seated in the chair with Nellore cradled in her arms.

"Ye've been busy, my dear."

Shoney looked up to see Ronan staring down at her with a bemused, and slightly bewildered, look on his face. She spoke of how she came to find Nellore and gave her husband an account of her vision of their clan's badge, the pine branch, bursting into flame.

He paced the length of the hall, clearly needing time to absorb all she had said. After a while, he looked at Shoney, his face strained with frustration.

"But what is the significance of your vision? What does it mean?" he asked.

Shoney laid the sleeping infant on a pallet and walked over to where Ronan stood, wrapping her arms around his waist.

"I know not the fullness of meaning. The only thing I am certain of is that the destiny of our clan and the destiny of Nellore are somehow crossed."

Chapter Two
Isle of Mull, Scotland
1306

"I feel as though I've come home, Logan," Garik called out over the din of the blistering coastal winds that barreled off the Sound of Mull and tore across the moors. "Too long has it been since I've seen these shores." His appreciative gaze scanned the sea as they rode parallel to the edge of the north cliffs. Rising in his seat, he peered down past the steep ledge to the breaking waves below.

"Ye *have* come home," Logan replied.

Garik nodded, realizing his friend was right. Neither Logan nor he had been born on Mull, but both had spent their formative years on the Isle. Logan's silvery eyes crinkled with pleasure. "We are both blessed to have two homes: the homes of our fathers," Logan said. Then dropping his reins and raising his arms as though to encompass the surrounding moors and rocky cliffs, he said, "and here, the Isle of Mull."

"We are losing one of the horses," Garik said, pointing to a grey palfrey that had stopped to graze at some brittle autumn grasses. Logan turned his horse around, trotted over to the lagging beast and grabbed hold of the reins, urging him to rejoin the five other horses they had brought along on their journey.

When Logan fell in line with Garik once more, they continued forward. Garik inhaled the salty air. Seven years had passed since he had fostered under the care of Ronan, the chieftain of the Mull MacKinnon. He had arrived on Mull when he was seven, just a few short months after Logan had arrived from his home on Skye. For five years, they had trained together and had become like brothers. As much as Garik had missed his birth home on the Orkney Islands, he had regretted leaving Mull on his twelfth birthday when his fostering years had ended. Logan, as the heir to the MacKinnon chiefdom, had remained on Mull. Garik was not certain whether Logan had ever returned to Skye. As the future chieftain of the MacKinnon, Logan's place was beside his laird.

As he once more stared out over the grey, choppy seas, Garik's mind drifted toward his birth home off the northeasterly tip of Scotland. His people celebrated their own unique culture, carved out of centuries of exposure to two powerful nations. The Scots and Norse had collided on the Orkney Islands, merging the peoples and cultures together over centuries, and from out of that mix had sprung forth, Norn, a language spoken only by those who dwelled on the Orkney Islands.

Garik laughed out loud remembering how his strange accent had always been a point of interest to his Scottish family on Mull. To someone who might not know better, the singsong lilt of his voice sounded like he was a Viking, which would not be entirely wrong. Like most Orcadians, he considered himself to be both Highlander and Viking, although loyalty to

Scotland had grown ever since King Haakon of Norway had been driven out of the Hebrides at the Battle of Largs.

Garik's grandfather, Aidan MacKinnon, hailed from Mull and had fought alongside his clansmen at that bloody battle where the winds blew with fury and storms ravaged both armies. Scotland had been the hard-won victor in the end, sending the Viking king home with a broken and diminished fleet of warships. Garik's grandfather had spoken often of that fierce battle, instilling within him a deeply rooted loyalty to Scotland.

Like so many of his kin on the Orkney Islands, Garik's heart longed for the day when Scotland would claim their small cluster of islands within its boundaries. England, however, stood in the way of that dream, and more than that, it threatened the well-being of his Scottish family, which was the precise reason he had arrived on Mull yesterday, along with ten other warriors from his small village of Kirkwall. They came to join with the Mull MacKinnon in their support of Robert the Bruce, the newly crowned King of Scotland.

"We are nearly to the Cave MacKinnon," Garik said, observing the softer lay of the land as the cliffs diminished in height, bringing the narrow, rocky coast below into closer reach. "Angus Og MacDonald's secrecy is enough to drive a man to madness."

"Aye," Logan agreed, "but his message was clear. He planned to make port in the Cave MacKinnon and wait for escort to Gribun. I do not ken why he guards this particular visit to Mull with such secrecy. In the past, he has always sailed straight into port."

Garik knew Angus Og MacDonald only by reputation. According to Ronan and every other warrior from Mull for that matter, a more level-headed warrior Garik would never meet. Angus Og had begun life as the youngest son of Angus Mor MacDonald who was reputed to have been a fierce warlord in his day. All of Angus Og's brothers had met some dark end, however, leaving Angus Og to inherit his father's title. He was now Lord of Islay and the wealthiest and most powerful chieftain in the west. A longtime and staunch supporter of Robert the Bruce, Angus Og had been made one of the Bruce's lieutenants.

As they neared the Cave MacKinnon, Garik found himself growing increasingly excited. He once again wondered about Angus Og's secret mission. Little could be gleaned from the missive he had sent in the hand of a messenger, who Logan had described as having been as tight-lipped as the parchment he had delivered with its few vague scribbles. A day and location and a request for extra horses was all the letter contained.

He remembered from his exploration of the isle as a boy that the Cave MacKinnon was tall and deep and teemed with ocean waves, even when the tide was at its lowest. Already he was impressed by Angus Og's cunning. Hiding a ship from view was no easy matter, but Angus Og's plan would no doubt work. Whatever he transported on his ship that he wanted to remain a secret would be well concealed within the deep cavern.

Logan reined in his horse and slid from his mount. "The horses cannot follow where we go," he said.

Garik dismounted and peered down the ravine to the wisp of shoreline, which had been swallowed up by the ever encroaching and then receding waves. The rest of the shore he assumed had been consumed long ago by the rough seas that beat the coast of Mull in winter.

"I'll race you," Garik jested as he carefully picked his way down the treacherous slope toward the meager coast below. A rock shifted beneath his foot and he skidded down, grappling at the cliff wall to stop his accelerated descent. Disturbed gravel rained down, pelting the advancing waves. With a sigh of relief, he twisted his neck to look up at Logan. "You were almost stuck with the task of fishing me out of the water," he said.

"'Tis more likely ye'd be swimming home." Logan said, his easy laughter taunting Garik, but then his voice dropped slightly. "Ye ken what I hope?"

"No, I cannot even venture a guess," Garik muttered, giving most of his attention to the precarious climb.

"I hope Angus Og packed light for this journey, or else I fear I will have to shirk the demands of hospitality and force him to haul his own effects to the surface."

It was Garik's turn to hoot with laughter, but once more he lost control and skidded forward. When he came to a halt, a sideways smile curved his lips as he twisted to say to Logan, "No more jests until we reach solid ground, or else we will both plummet to the water and all hospitality will be forgotten."

Garik stepped onto what he realized was less of a shoreline and more a simple ledge. Then he shimmied against the cliff wall in the direction of the cave. Being in the lead when they at last reached the opening, Garik turned so his stomach pressed against the cliffside and peered inside. His eyes widened with surprise when he met the gazes of five men awaiting their arrival. They stood on a dry ledge within the cave; however, the waterline on the cave wall proved that come high tide the ledge would disappear beneath the waves. Deeper within, Garik could just make out the shadow of a vessel that would remain well concealed from any other ships passing near to shore.

"Greetings," Garik said. No sooner did the word leave his lips, then three arrow tips were aimed at his face. His eyes scanned the men threatening his life. With their plaids and long, wild hair, Garik knew straightaway they were Highlanders. The other two men, who stood alongside the Highlanders, resembled Garik in dress. Like him, they both wore long woolen tunics over dark pants with leather jerkins belted at the waist, but one of the men's clothing was finer than the others. He was clearly a man of wealth and importance.

"My name is Garik Mackinnon," he said, smiling. "You do not need your weapons. I've come with Logan MacKinnon." The men made no move to lower their arrows. Garik cleared his throat as he considered what to say next. "We've been sent by our laird to escort you to Gribun."

"I've not met ye before, Viking," one of the Highlanders growled. He had brown hair and steady blue eyes that bore no hint of the malice that laced his voice.

"You must be Angus Og MacDonald." Garik said as he continued to smile in greeting. The Highlander's eyes narrowed but he neither confirmed nor denied the claim. Garik decided at that moment that the future chieftain of the MacKinnon was better suited for welcoming visitors to Mull. "I suggest we be properly introduced, but..." he said as he began to step slowly backwards. "That honor I will leave for Logan. If you will just excuse me, I will try to let him pass without the two of us taking an unscheduled swim. The ledge we stand on is a trifle narrow," he explained before turning back to Logan.

"Your friends do not like me," Garik said. "I think they may be under the impression that I am Viking."

"Well, 'tis because ye are a Viking," Logan said, his silver eyes alight with laughter.

"Saints above," Garik countered with a chuckle. "How many times must I tell you I'm an Orcadian?"

"Aye, I ken. I ken," Logan said as he picked his way around Garik and disappeared into the cave."

Garik returned to the horses and waited for what he hoped would be more peaceable company.

When Logan and his five new companions at last stood before Garik, they continued to eye him with suspicion. "Before we introduce ourselves, I would know his name," the fierce Highlander said, looking pointedly at Garik.

"He is Garik MacKinnon. His grandfather, Aidan MacKinnon, hails from Mull and was our chieftain's closest friend in their youth. He left Mull many years ago, however, to make a home on the Orkney Islands," Logan said.

"Why did this Aidan leave Mull in the first place? He was not dishonored?" Angus Og asked, glowering now at Garik.

"Nay," Garik said. "'Twas the love of a woman. What else has the power to compel a man to leave his home?"

"Garik is no stranger to Mull," Logan interjected. "He fostered here in his youth. Yesterday marked his return to our shores. He has come back to Mull so that he might join our cause." Logan rested his hand on Garik's shoulder as he met the Highlander's gaze with a challenge. "He came to answer *your* call to arms, Angus Og."

Garik had guessed correctly back in the cave. The man he had thought to be Angus Og stepped forward. He was not nearly as tall as Garik nor was he as broad, but his gaze held a confidence and an intelligence that inspired Garik.

"Ye look like a Viking," Angus Og said. "Ye sound like one too, but ye keep good company. If ye fostered under Ronan, then I ken you must be a fine warrior." Angus Og smiled slightly. "I am Angus Og MacDonald, Lord of Islay. I am joined by two members of my clan. This here is Lachlann," Angus said, gesturing to a stout warrior with bright red hair to his left. "And Hamish." He pointed to an older warrior with long, graying hair and a scar that ran from the top of his brow, through his eye, which appeared to be rendered useless, and down to the middle of his cheek.

Garik nodded at both men.

Then Logan stepped forward. "Ye've now been introduced to my guest, but what manner of men have ye brought?" Logan said, jerking his head toward the two lowlanders who stood silently behind the MacDonalds.

"'Tis my honor to introduce Lord James Douglas, one of our king's lieutenants," Angus Og said. The younger and less finely dressed of the two men stepped forward and dipped his head in greeting.

"I bid ye welcome," Logan said.

"Indeed, you are most welcome," Garik said with a bow. Now that he had a proper look at James, he was struck by the man's youthful eyes. "Forgive my candor, Lord Douglas," Garik began, "but you seem rather young to be a lieutenant."

James smiled at Garik, but it was the wealthy man at his side who stepped forward with an answer. "He is one and twenty, no doubt only a year or two older than both of you, but let it be known that I trust no one so well as I do James. His instincts and mind for strategy have no equal. If you have come, young Garik MacKinnon, late of the Orkney Islands, to join my cause, know this—you will be taking your orders from him."

"Your cause?" Garik said, his eyes wide. He whirled around and met Logan's equally stunned gaze.

A slight smile played at Angus Og's lips. "Ye've not let me finish the introductions." He turned and swept his arm in a grand gesture toward the man who Logan and Garik now knew to be the king of Scotland. "Before ye stands Robert the Bruce," Angus Og said. Then he turned back to face Logan and Garik. "Men, ye owe him your allegiance."

Garik and Logan both dropped to their knees, folding their hands as though in prayer, and vowed to be true and faithful to their king.

The Bruce accepted their homage and bid them rise once more.

"Has the time come?" Garik asked. "Is that why you are here? Do we go to battle?"

Garik looked to his king, but it was James who answered. "Aye. War is at hand, and we've something special planned for the Mull MacKinnon."

Chapter Three

Riding in the lead, Garik was the first to crest the steep hillside that led down into a valley on the outskirts of Gribun. Scanning the huts scattered about the plain, Garik raised his hand to signal danger. Horses grazed in a distant field while five warriors crawled on their bellies toward one of the huts with blades drawn.

"MacLeans," Logan growled. He reached behind his back to free his blade, but the king stayed his hand.

"Hold, Logan. The MacLean's son, Balfour, swore fealty to me at Scone two years ago. Make my presence known and I shall restore a peace."

Garik had no interest in exposing the king's presence on the isle to the blackguard MacLean, and by the looks on the rest of the men's faces, they agreed.

"Nay, my liege. I dare not test the MacLean's love for ye against his hatred for my clan. Our feud is old," Logan said.

"I implore ye to heed Logan's caution," Angus Og said. "'Tis a band of five men. Wait here. We shall subdue them with ease and then continue on to Gribun."

"Five men and one lass," the Bruce said.

"What?" both Garik and Logan said in unison as they whirled around. A lass with wild, black hair came out from behind the long, thatched hut, charging toward the MacLeans on

14

a fine, black palfrey. She reached behind her back and drew a sword that she brandished high and from her lips came forth a chilling battle cry.

"God's blood, Nellore," Logan cursed as he kicked his horse in the flanks.

"He appears to be familiar with the lass," James said to the king with a grin.

"Did I not tell ye of the fierce Mull MacKinnons?" Angus Og chuckled. "Even their women are cutthroat."

"That is no woman. She is naught but a wee lass," Garik said. With his eye trained on the girl, he raced after Logan, sounding the battle cry of the MacKinnon. He could not believe one lass could be so spirited or so deadly. As soon as she was close enough, she leapt from her horse, pinning a man more than twice her size to the ground—not with her weight, for she was a wisp of a lass. It was the steel pressed against the vein in his neck that made him lie so still and her green eyes that flashed with blood lust.

"Move and I will cut ye open," she taunted.

Garik's eyes widened with astonishment.

"For the love of all things decent, Nellore. I did not teach ye that," Logan said with a grimace. Then he turned to look down upon the MacLean warrior who lay disarmed at his feet. "We will spill no blood here today, but listen well, ye spineless coward. Any crime carried out by a MacLean on MacKinnon soil shall be returned ten-fold."

The enemy tried to struggle to his feet, but Logan pressed him back into the dirt with his foot. "Ye can leave the same way ye came—on your bellies like snakes. Now, be gone from our land."

The lass replaced her blade in the scabbard strapped to her back with what appeared to be a look of regret upon her face. She then joined Logan in watching the progress of the MacLeans as they scrambled toward their horses. It was not until the warriors were mounted and racing back to their own territory that Logan turned to address the child.

"I did not teach ye to wield that blade so that ye could put yourself in harm's way," Logan said, his silver eyes flashing. Garik was reminded of Logan's grandmother, the lady of their clan, whose coloring Logan had inherited. On the few occasions Garik had crossed the Lady Bridget in his youth, her queer, silver eyes had gleamed like polished coins just as Logan's did now. Equally as difficult to offend as his grandmother, it was not often that Garik saw Logan's eyes flash, and although it was a chilling sight, apparently, Nellore thought differently. She appeared unaffected. The scowl that distorted Logan's handsome features would have made many men step down, but the recipient of his anger was no man. Garik choked back laughter as she turned and flung a finger in Logan's face.

"Ye taught me to defend myself and my own, which is what I just did," she snapped.

"What ye just did was almost get yourself killed. Ye aimed to take on five grown men. Ye have skill, Nellore, but ye're a child," Logan said.

"And a lass," Garik could not resist adding. Angry, green eyes flashed his way before they turned back to glare again at Logan. "I've twelve years to my credit. I'm no longer a child. Besides, I intended to ride for aid, but then I saw ye. So, I turned my horse around and attacked."

Logan raised a skeptical brow.

"I speak the truth," she said. Several moments passed while she withstood the might of Logan's scrutiny, but she gave him no further opportunity to scold her. Garik grinned with pleasure when, apparently having decided the matter should be dismissed, Nellore threw her arms around Logan's neck.

"Where have ye been, Logan? I've not seen ye for days and days."

Garik could not believe Nellore's transformation from shield maiden to child. An endless string of questions gushed forth from her lips at a dizzying rate.

"We've been on a hunting party, and then yesterday Garik's ship drew into port so I've not had a chance to visit ye. Do ye remember Garik at all?"

She turned to scrutinize Garik with wide, green eyes and a face smudged with dirt. She continued to stare at him but shook her head in reply.

"You may not remember me, lass, but I remember you. You used to follow us about, but not with a rag baby in your arms like the other girls," Garik said, laughing. "No, not you. You would proudly tout a wooden sword in your tough grip. It would seem little has changed."

Nellore continued to stare at him. He thought he might have angered her youthful heart with his earlier quip, but then at last she spoke. "I do not remember ever meeting ye, but I do like how ye speak. What are ye then?" Suddenly, her eyes danced with excitement. "Are ye a Viking?"

"Not exactly," he replied with a smile. Then Logan cut in.

"What are ye doing out here alone?" Logan asked.

"I was visiting Mary," she said.

"But who rode out here with ye? Ye ken ye aren't meant to—" A throat clearing behind them pulled Garik and Logan's attention away from Nellore.

"Logan," the Bruce said. "Will you not make introductions?"

"Of course, my liege," he said as he turned Nellore about to face the king. "Your majesty, this is Nellore, daughter of Duncan and Brenna MacKinnon. She is my sister in all ways but blood." He then motioned to the Bruce. "Nellore, ye're standing before the king of Scotland."

Garik had to suppress a chuckle when Nellore dipped into a confused curtsy. She truly was an impressive sight. Her hair fell about her head in wild disarray. Thick brows framed what he decided would be lovely eyes when she was grown. A shadow of dirt seemed to cover every inch of her.

"Is it your practice to train your women in skilled combat?" the Bruce asked Logan.

Garik turned an eager ear to hear Logan's response.

"Over this last decade, by the urging of my grandmother, the Lady Bridget, all of our women have become trained archers. She thought it wrong to leave them defenseless if our men were overrun in battle. Some are more capable than others, but all are able to hit their mark. The bow is where their training begins and ends. Nellore is an exception," Logan smiled sheepishly. "I am to blame for her skill with a sword."

"'Tis just like ye, Logan, to claim ownership over what is mine," Nellore said, scowling. She turned to the king. "He trained me, but only because I showed such promise."

"Indeed," the King smiled. "A braver or cleverer lass I've not had the pleasure of meeting, and I am the father of three fine daughters." The Bruce extended his hand toward Nellore. "May I hold your sword?"

Garik laughed outright when she clutched her sword tighter and retreated steps away from the men. Once again, her green eyes narrowed on him. "The king only wishes to admire your blade, little one," Garik said.

Much to Garik's surprise, she stretched to her full height and stalked right up to him. "I am many things, sir—disobedient, willful, ill-mannered, and ugly, but little I am not."

She stared up at him, her bright green eyes unafraid amid tangled black hair. Indeed, she nearly came up to his chest, which was impressive given he was tall and she still not fully grown. He scrutinized her features once more: thick brows, pert nose, and wide full lips. She bore the awkwardness of youth, but he predicted one day she would be an unusual beauty. Her features would never appear refined, but she would captivate those men daring enough to see beyond convention.

"You are a tall, fine lass," Garik said softly. "Now, give the king your sword."

A blush tinted her cheeks as she handed her blade to the Bruce. Still, she guarded her weapon with possessive eyes. Like most warriors, Garik could tell she did not like another's hand gripping her sword. "What a queer, little minx you've become," Garik said with admiration. Her eyes tore away from her blade and met his with naked aggression. He raised his hands in mock surrender. "My words were not meant to sting," he said. "I think you are the finest, wee lass I've ever had the pleasure of meeting. I only wish my own sister had a drop of your gumption. She is as thin and flimsy as a morning breeze." At his words, those green eyes softened, and her wide, full lips parted as a dazzling smile stretched across her face. Her smile nigh stole his breath. "You are prettier than you think, child," he said.

"I'm not a child," she declared, thrusting out her chin.

"Ten and two does not a woman make," he replied.

"Enough with your frivolities," the king interrupted. "Garik, you are undermining the courage of my newest warrior."

Nellore's head jerked up and she stared at her king with mouth agape.

"'Tis a fine blade," the Bruce said as he slashed the air with her sword.

"I had it made to suit her," Logan said. "Although her father was displeased to say the least, as was my chieftain. 'Tis lighter and shorter than a normal blade, yet still quite strong."

Her fingers reached out and stroked across the steel of her sword. "Am I truly counted among your warriors?" she asked of the king.

"Aye, lass. You are a shield maiden of Scotland," he answered.

"Then I can march with ye?" she said.

The Bruce chuckled and ruffled her mussed hair. "Nay, lass. Mayhap when you are grown. For now, I need you here to protect your kinfolk while Logan, Garik, and the others are away."

"Do not fash yourself, lass." It was Hamish who spoke. Garik turned, surprised to hear the older man speak for the first time. His fierce scar might have scared another lass, but not Nellore. She looked up at Hamish with hopeful eyes. "I could be your squire," she said.

Hamish laughed. "I'm no pampered knight," he said. Then turning to the king and James, he muttered, "begging your pardon, my lords." Then he turned back to Nellore. "I too must remain behind."

A loud sigh of dejection passed from her lips as her head hung low. Clearly, she had hoped Hamish had found a solution that had her marching off to battle.

"But ye can help me defend your home. 'Tis why I've come. To offer the Mull MacKinnon my sword and one good eye for the defense of your people while so many of your warriors are called away."

Logan put his arm around her shoulder. "Ye know ye cannot go to battle, Nellore," he said. Then he swept her up in his arms and spun her around until she laughed with girlish delight. "But ye still wield the fastest blade on Mull," he said, laughing.

"Faster even than ye?" she said.

"Faster even than Garik," Logan said. Garik smiled at Logan, remembering how he had bested the future chieftain that morning when they sparred.

Nellore scrambled out of Logan's arms and hurried to Garik's side. Her gaze traveled over his leather jerkin and wool pants. She liked the look of him. His hair was as black as the chough bird's feathers, and his skin was stark white like the snow that still clung to Benmore Mountain. But it was his eyes that made her forget to breathe. They were ice blue in color but held none of winter's cold. In fact, they shone with warmth and humor.

The Bruce drew her gaze away from Garik's when he stepped forward. "Nellore, I am compelled to tell you that if you were my daughter, I would chain you to a chair in your room until you were old enough to wed. But since you do not belong to me, I choose instead to encourage your fierce nature. I can only pray the men under my command have even half your valor."

Nellore beamed as she mounted her horse. "Did ye hear what the king said?" she whispered in the palfrey's ear. Her horse skippered beneath her as powerful and hell bound with vigor as she.

She galloped across the moors toward Gribun with the men at her side. Exhilaration coursed through her akin to nothing she had ever experienced. With the king and so many warriors surrounding her, it was easy to imagine she was every part the warrior of her dreams. She met Garik's smiling eyes and laughed. Beyond anything, she wished she were grown and could fight alongside her king and kinsmen.

Chapter Four

The MacKinnon warriors were in the midst of training when they approached Gribun. Garik watched as each man balanced a massive caber in their arms while they crossed the wide plain. Youthful memories of dragging his weary and aching body into the great hall of Dun Ara Castle only to fall into an exhausted stupor during the evening meal rushed to the fore of his mind. By the bone-tired expressions worn on all the warriors' faces, he could surmise that Ronan was as ruthless as ever. According to his grandfather, Aidan, Ronan had always pushed the men to the point of breaking. More than once, Aidan had affectionately referred to Ronan as 'that tyrant'.

Now, at nearly seventy-one years of age, Ronan's strength had at last diminished. While Garik watched the training, he noted that Ronan did not participate in some of the drills; whereas, when he had fostered with the MacKinnon, Ronan would have matched his warriors move for move. Still, for a man of Ronan's advanced years, Garik was impressed by the drills his trimmer yet still sinewy physique managed to complete.

Garik chuckled as Ronan barked at the men to keep moving. One thing he could say for certain was that the years had done nothing to soften Ronan's voice. But no one uttered a single complaint. Everyone knew that Ronan's unrelenting demands and brutal tactics were behind the renowned skill of the Mull MacKinnon warriors. Garik did not doubt that Ronan's despotic role on the training fields and the resulting discipline of his men were the very reasons the king of Scotland stood nearby watching the Mull warriors with avid interest.

Much to the apparent relief of his men, Ronan dismissed the warriors to the keep and strode toward his audience. He first approached Angus Og. Garik could tell by the warmth of Ronan's greeting that he held the laird of the Clan MacDonald in high esteem. Angus Og returned Ronan's welcome with the same open affection, and then straightaway he introduced the Bruce.

A flash of surprise passed over Ronan's face, and a glint of excitement lit his amber eyes. He knelt and kissed the Bruce's hand. "Long have we prayed for a true king to claim Scotland's throne," he said. Then Ronan stood and introduced the man at his side.

"This is my second in command, Duncan MacKinnon," Ronan said.

Duncan came forward and knelt before the king, also swearing his allegiance. When Duncan rose to his feet, Nellore rushed to his side. He smiled down at her. "Look at how filthy ye are, lass, and in front of the king no less," he said before pressing a kiss to her head. "Ye've met my eldest lass then?" Duncan said to the Bruce.

"Aye. In fact, I had the privilege of observing her skill with a blade," the king replied.

Garik did not envy the look Logan received from Duncan before Duncan turned his attention once more to the Bruce. "I face the English without fear, for I ken Nellore will be the death of me."

Duncan continued to lament Nellore's preference for daggers and swords over cooking ladles and sewing needles, but Garik could sense underneath it all, he was proud of his daughter's exceptional skills.

"Let us retire to the keep," Ronan said. "I admit I grow impatient to hear the news that brings the king of Scotland to my shore."

THE BRUCE STOOD AT the head of a long, rough-hewn wooden table that stretched nigh the length of the great hall. His hands rested on the surface as he leaned forward, meeting the gaze of every single warrior, one by one. "If we are to reclaim the glory of a united and free Scotland, I need warriors with skill and fury in their hearts to match the demand of my ambition. I need warriors willing to sacrifice everything to win—their lives, even their honor."

"Your majesty," James interrupted, "forgive me, but mayhap, you should start at the beginning."

The Bruce nodded. "You are right as always, James. Before I ask them to break knightly codes of conduct, they should know why."

Ronan was quick to reply. "I would hear your tale, my liege, but know this—there are no knights on Mull, only warriors."

"It would seem I've come to the right place," the Bruce said, smiling. Then he stood and began to pace the room as he spoke. "Two years ago, King Edward gave Aymer de Valence, the Earl of Pembroke, orders to raise the dragon banner against me."

"What does that mean?" Garik asked.

It was Ronan who answered. "It means Valence was ordered to give no quarter, no mercy, take no prisoners. The dragon banner does not honor knightly codes."

The Bruce nodded. Then he closed his eyes, seemingly to gather his thoughts.

Silence resounded in the great hall as all eyes turned expectantly to the one man with the will and bloodline to unite a nation divided and fight for Scotland's independence.

At length, the king spoke. "With an army of more than four thousand strong, we marched to Perth to call Valence out to battle, but he refused." His lips curled with contempt. "And so, I led the men to Methven to make camp." He closed his eyes once more, but this time Garik could tell he did so to garner his strength. With a deep breath, he opened his eyes and moved to stand before James. "Lord Douglas had advised me to heavily guard the camp, arguing Valence was not to be trusted. But my foolish heart still beat to the rhythm of valor and honor and the knightly codes Lord Valence himself had also sworn to uphold." Disdain flavored the king's voice, leading Garik to guess the Bruce's anger was as much with himself as with Valence.

"I was mistaken," the Bruce said. "Just as James had predicted, Valence attacked. Under the cover of darkness, the enemy gathered around our camp in the night, surrounding us. Then, like savage beasts, dark shadows came alive and devoured our defenseless camp. My men were pulled from their sleep and butchered. Many fled into the woods, but there was no place to run. The trees released only their screams. Surrounded, outnumbered, and caught unprepared, my hard-earned army was slaughtered."

Garik watched pain and regret pass like shadows over his contrite leader's face. He knew the Bruce blamed himself for the death of so many. Such a burden he could only imagine would weigh heavily on one's soul.

"They captured my nephew, Thomas Randolf. I can only pray he lives, imprisoned somewhere despite Valence's order to show no quarter. They took my wife and daughters shortly after that. They are being held in a convent. Those of us that survived were forced west to take refuge. I believed the mountains of Argyle would cradle my broken army. The narrow, steep passes would keep Valence's cavalry at bay, but once more I was proven wrong. As we climbed higher and higher, a battle cry descended from near the top of the summit. Hell rained down upon our battle-weary bodies. You see, I had underestimated the English king's reach. The clan MacDougall attacked, and my tired army was no match for the fierce Highlanders. The only reason James and I still live is because of Angus Og. At the time of the attack, he had been leading his men in a march to join my army. Crossing the Argyle Mountains on his way east, he heard the battle and took up the fight, forcing the Mac-Dougalls to scatter once more up the mountain pass."

Angus Og's fist slammed down on the table, surprising Garik with his impassioned display. "Long has my clan suffered injury at the hand of the MacDougall," Angus Og said. Then he turned to the king and vowed, "We will put an end to their treachery before the last battle in this war is fought."

The Bruce grabbed up his cup and raised it high. "You will have your chance. To the Clan MacDonald," the Bruce said.

"To the Clan MacDonald," echoed the men, raising their cups in Angus Og's honor.

Lowering his cup to the table, the king scanned the room, again looking every man in the eye. The Bruce's steel gaze locked with Garik's, and he felt the urgency of the moment like a jolt of power course through him. "When the MacDougalls fled, we were too broken to celebrate our own salvation. It was a turning point in our quest for independence. I had to decide. Had all been for naught? Had those men, my followers, my family suffered in vain? For a time, I saw no hope."

Duncan jumped to his feet. "But there is always hope," he cried. "I've been hungry for English blood since witnessing the massacre at Berwick. We must never surrender."

James stood then, his gaze fixed on Duncan. "I was at Berwick," he said. "My father, William Douglas, was the city's governor. For two days, my little brothers and sister and I huddled together in a high tower, listening to the endless screams of the dying. As my father's heir, he secreted me away from the keep on the third day. I was taken to France where I remained hidden in a monastery. I was not yet ten at the time."

"Your father was a great man," Duncan said. "If memory serves, he was one of the first of Scotland's nobles to support William Wallace."

"Aye, that he was," James said.

"Your mention of William Wallace in a way brings us to why we are here," the Bruce said. "Angus Og was good enough to hide me away while we recouped men and considered how best to proceed. Both he and James served as my council during that time. After months of deliberation, we were able to draw one indisputable conclusion—we cannot win this war."

An uproar erupted as the men lunged to their feet, urging their king not to surrender his quest, but the Bruce silenced their protest with a raised hand. "I speak the truth. We cannot win by conventional means." Then he nodded towards James who stood and took the Bruce's place at the head of the table.

"We are smaller and have fewer resources. The odds are not in our favor. If we bring this fight to the battlefield, the open plain, we will lose," James said flatly. But then he traded his grim expression for a smile as he continued. "Now that we've looked honestly at our weaknesses, let it be understood, we will win this war."

James walked around the table as he spoke. "Wallace brought England to its knees because he instilled fear into the heart of our enemy. He refused to play by the rules, and neither shall we. The slaughtering of our men at Methven was two years ago. We've since met Valence in battle, but with a vastly different outcome."

Garik leaned forward in his seat eager to hear the young lieutenant's report.

"Valence marched with a massive army whose sole purpose was to find our location and destroy us once and for all. We took position on Loudoun Hill, knowing that bogs lined that section of road. Then we waited, hidden among the trees. When they passed, we ambushed their march. The narrow passage restricted how many men Valence could deploy. His mighty army was nothing more than a trickling stream." A glint of triumph lit James's eyes as he continued. "They panicked. Without a conventional battlefield, they dissolved into chaos. While we came together to form a Schiltron—a great circle. Marching in a tight cluster with long spears and our shields permanently presented, we resembled an armored animal with bristling spikes. Holding formation, we advanced and fought with such ferocity that they fled. Victory was ours."

Roars of triumph thundered throughout the hall. After a time, James held out his hands to silence the men. "We can celebrate when we've truly won. 'Tis only the beginning. For now, the Bruce is going to lead our ever-growing army onward and cut away at Edward's forces using what we've come to view as our greatest weapon, our superior knowledge of Scotland's countryside. He will use the hills, the rivers, and the forests to our end. He will burn fields and kill livestock as our army advances to deny the English fresh supplies. As for me, I'm going to break off and focus on bringing down the Scottish strongholds still held under English authority." James moved to stand before Angus Og. "I told the Lord of Islay that I needed a small band of men as fierce and cunning as Wallace. He told me I could live ten lifetimes and never again encounter finer warriors than those found on the Isle of Mull. I ask you all now, was Angus Og correct?"

In reply, the hall echoed with the battle cry of the MacKinnon.

"We will be outnumbered," James said. "A small band of men versus a well garrisoned castle, but we shall use stealth and cunning to take each stronghold, one by one. What say you, Ronan?" James asked as he stopped before the chieftain.

Ronan stood and stretched out his arms to include every Mull MacKinnon in his reply. "We shall not be sated until Edward of England and all his affiliates have been beaten, bled, and burned from this land," he roared. "We've been waiting for the true king to rise to power." His hand then clamped down on James's shoulder. "Ye arrived today on the shores of Mull looking for the best, and, by my trove, ye've found the best!"

Logan raised his cup. "Come," he said. "Feast with us, for we've much to celebrate."

"To new beginnings," Garik shouted before tipping his own cup.

The hall soon filled with villagers drawn to the celebration that had ensued. Garik's heart filled with merriment as he danced a reel, joining Logan and several beautiful lassies as they wove through the hall in circles while pipers played. After a time, the music changed, and a rich, braw voice drew his attention, uprooting all other thoughts.

Like a strong breeze it surrounded him and stole his breath. He opened his eyes to find what creature could croon with such feeling that it made his heart ache. He gasped with surprise. There by the fire, surrounded by a rapt audience, stood the child, Nellore. Her eyes squeezed shut, her hands clenched, and from her lips came forth a sound powerful and lush.

Her hair remained unkempt, falling in ragged curls about her waist, but her face shone clean and warm in the firelight. He joined many of the clan who sat enraptured while they listened to her croon each impassioned note. She surprised him when suddenly her eyes flew open and green fire met his. Her gaze bore into his soul as she continued to fill the night with her haunting song. He did not look away. Instead, he smiled and was given such a smile in return. Her expression held pure joy. It reached across the crowd and the fire and filled him with the same happiness.

Nellore sang from her heart. When she stood before her clan singing tales of battles won and lost, she never felt more alive. She used to watch her audience when she sang, but then one night she realized the warriors listened with their eyes closed. As she sang their stories, they relived the glory and sadness. It was then that she too began to close her eyes. She would imagine herself among the men, fighting for justice, fighting for those who could not. Pain would grip her heart while she lived a dream through her song. And when the music ended, and her voice trailed off, the pain grew for she knew that was all it would ever be—a dream.

She was not destined for battle. Her future resided in a cage of stone and peat. She would be like her mother, tied to the hearth and harvest. When she came of age, her sword would become a trinket to glimpse in the corner, and the part of her that in youth craved to fight would go unfulfilled until it was altogether forgotten.

When she sang that night and realized Garik, the Viking warrior, listened to her song, her heart filled with pride. Perhaps upon hearing her passion he would ask her to join his band of warriors. She closed her eyes as she finished, but when the song ended, he had already turned away. Sadness struck her heart. Nothing had changed.

The next day, the warriors left without Nellore in their number. Her da scooped her up into his arms, and she cried into his long, black hair.

"I ken ye cry because I'm leaving, but I also ken ye cry because ye're not."

She nodded her head. "God made me this way for a reason," she said. "Why would he grant me the will and the talent to learn and to fight if not to be given the chance?"

"His purpose for ye will be revealed in time, but ye're young. Even if ye were a lad, ye would still be too young to follow. Ye ken?"

She nodded, knowing he was right.

"Now look to your mum and how she suffers my absence. Think ye she could get by a day without ye?"

Her eyes burned with tears as she turned to look upon Brenna who stood by seemingly composed to all but those who knew her best. Her fists gripped her skirts, and her blue eyes fought against the fear that Nellore could tell threatened to consume her. Standing at her side was Nellore's little sister Rose whose straight, strawberry hair hid woeful eyes.

Duncan put Nellore down, and she soon found herself staring up into Logan's silver gaze. "Ye visit with Father Conall and keep up with your studies," he said.

"He promised to teach me French next, but I am not to tell anyone. He said 'tis a sin to teach a woman."

Garik appeared at her side just then. "If God didn't want you to learn, he would not have made you so bright. You are like a star in the darkness," he said.

She beamed at his praise. "Then I shall shine all the brighter to guide ye both home. Will ye come for me when I'm old enough," she said, shifting her pleading gaze between Logan and Garik. "At your side with my sword raised high is where I ought to be."

"We shall see, dear sister," Logan said before turning away.

Her brows came together, and her smile faded. Garik brushed a wayward lock of hair from her eyes. Then he smiled down at her. "You shall be a fierce woman when you've grown, a strong Scottish woman with talents you have yet to discover. And I shall be proud to call you friend," he said.

She smiled as he walked away, all the while his words echoing in her mind. *I shall be proud to call you friend.* He had given her hope about the woman she would one day become.

Chapter Five
Isle of Mull, Scotland
Summer 1311

The sun began its descent toward the vast ocean horizon. Golden tones shone against stark cliffs that towered above the rocky shoreline, lending their hard surfaces fleeting radiance while the day drew its last breath. Nellore peered into a tidal pool, studying her reflection before the approaching evening chased it away.

"What does she say to ye?"

She looked up and found Bridget standing before her. The water lapped at Bridget's toes and dampened the hem of her tunic.

"Nothing," she said, confused. "'Tis only I."

Bridget smiled. The creases around her eyes and lips reflected her age, at which Nellore could only guess. When faced with the question, Bridget always laughed and would say she had forgotten her age long ago. "I am not as old as the sun or the moon," she had often said. "And the mountains certainly precede me. But to the trees and heather I will always say that I believe I came first." For many years, Nellore had believed Bridget's claims and had stared at her in wonder, thinking she had seen the birth of the first tree.

Now, Nellore turned her eyes away from the lady of her clan and stared once more at herself in the still water.

"She will speak, dear one, if ye listen. She will reveal the truths hidden away in your heart, hidden even from yourself," Bridget said.

Nellore concentrated on the green eyes staring back at her. Her thick, black brows came together as she narrowed her gaze. With all her will she strained to hear, but her soul revealed nothing other than that which she already knew—longing...but for what?

She released a sigh as she stood and wrapped her arms around Bridget's frail shoulders.

"Were ye searching for me then?" she asked as she breathed in Bridget's scent and felt peace enter her soul.

"Aye, but my search was not long. I knew just where to find ye," Bridget said with a wink. "When I was a young woman, I too looked to the sea for answers. I hoped my heart's desire would wash up on shore. I was hungry like ye are now."

Nellore shook her head. "I've no appetite for food."

"'Tis not food ye hunger for," Bridget said with a mischievous glint in her silver eyes. "For some time now, I've watched ye staring off into the distance with so much longing. Your soul is famished."

Nellore shrugged. "I do not ken my own heart other than to know that I crave what I cannot have."

Bridget took her hand and they started off together down the coast in the direction of the village.

"Ye fill me with such wonder," Bridget said. "Ye possess boundless strength and talent and yet remain so humble. Ye've let go the stubbornness of youth, and ye've grown in grace. If only I had been so smart. Pride caused me to stumble as a young woman, but then Ronan suffered from the same ailment. Neither of us could get out of our own way, and fall we did. Fortunately, however, we landed on each other."

Nellore laughed. "Ye mean fell in love with each other."

"Aye, we did that too," Bridget said with a chuckle. "But what is it that *ye* crave?"

"I'm not entirely certain. There is that part of me that still holds on to my childish dream of valor I suppose. Do not think me ungrateful, Bridget, because I ken my life is blessed, and I love this island. The forests, the moors, the cliffs, the waves—they are a part of me. But there are times I wish to leave. I wish to be with Da and Logan and Garik. I wish to join up and fight for Scotland."

"Do you ken what you would risk?" Bridget asked.

She felt the sting of tears, and she turned away from Bridget's knowing silver eyes to stare back out to sea. "Aye, I ken, and mayhap my courage would fail me, but..." Her voice trailed off. She shook her head, dismissing her own foolishness.

"Speak your mind, Nellore. 'Tis I. Ye're one of the few in this world to ken all my secrets." This was true. The clan believed Bridget was a healer from Skye who had come to Mull as a young woman and won the heart of Ronan, their future chieftain. In truth, Bridget's real name was Shoney, and she had never lived anywhere except Mull.

Before Ronan stumbled upon her by chance in the woods, Shoney had lived in isolation, disguised as the fearsome Witch of Dervaig. It was with a heavy heart that Shoney had worn the tattered cloak of the Witch, but it was all she had ever known. Her mother had worn the very same cloak and her mother's mother, going back centuries, all to escape harassment from the clan, for there was another little-known fact about the clan's lady: she was a pagan. The women of Shoney's descent had suffered through prejudice and persecution for their continued belief in the gods of the land, sea, and sky. It was only when they began donning the terrific cloak of the Witch that the clan had let them be. Over time, the legend of the Witch of Dervaig was born. The clan had feared her above all else, and the explanation given to her longevity—that she had sold her soul to Satan.

When Shoney's mother lived, she and her mother would take turns walking the moors beneath the cloak, scaring every clansman, woman, and child who passed by. But life took a vastly different turn when Ronan saw the young Shoney cast off the hood of her cloak to take aim at a deer in the woods. He fell in love with the mysterious silver-eyed lass. It was Ronan who convinced Shoney to take on a new identity so that she might be welcomed by the clan. And so, Shoney became Bridget, the lady of the Mull MacKinnon, loved by all. Only Ronan; Nellore's mother, Brenna; and Anna, who was one of Bridget's daughters, knew Bridget's true past. Even Bridget's other children remained ignorant of the truth. Bridget had confided in her daughter, Anna, only because Anna had inherited Bridget's gift of sight. Like her mother before her, Bridget had visions of the future.

Nellore pulled Bridget to a halt and looked down into her silver eyes. "Why must ye continue to deny who ye really are?

So many years have passed, a lifetime of years. I believe the clan is ready to embrace the truth."

"Bless ye," Bridget said as she reached out to grasp Nellore's hand. "Ye're young and full of conviction. Whereas I am old and still unconvinced the clan is ready to embrace a pagan woman with the gift of sight who used to masquerade as a terrible witch, believed to have sold her soul to Satan."

"Och, Shoney, when ye put it like that it does seem impossible."

"That is the truth. That is how the clan will see me if ever they learn who I really am, and call me, Bridget. Secrets are best kept when they are kept all the time."

Nellore nodded and pressed a kiss to Bridget's cheek. "Can I ask ye something?"

Bridget smiled her consent.

"Was it hard to leave your old life behind?"

Bridget turned her gaze out to the churning sea. "Three years before Ronan and I fell in love my mother passed away. I was alone in a way ye could never understand. 'Twas as though I did not even exist. Nay, in the end it was not hard to give up my old life. Now, giving up my name—that was an altogether different matter. That was hard. Shoney was the name my mother gave me. I felt as though I had betrayed her when I gave it up."

"Do ye still feel that way?" Nellore asked.

Bridget shrugged. "My mother would be proud of my life. That is all that matters. Now, enough talk about me. I am old. My life holds few questions these days. But what of ye? Out with it, lass. Speak to me."

"Oh, Bridget, why must ye always see straight into my soul? Is it your gift?"

"Nay, my love. Ye wear your heart and soul on your sleeve, Nellore."

Nellore took a deep breath. Then she blurted, "Do ye see my hands?" She thrust them out in front of her. Like the rest of her, they were large and powerful. She towered above the other women in the clan and several of the men. Her shoulders tightened, pulling the fabric of her tunic taut around the muscles in her arms.

"This body was not made to tend fires and mend tunics. Do not misunderstand me. I am honored to be a woman of my clan, to aid my mother in these ways. 'Tis just that when my hands grip the hilt of a sword it feels like destiny. My body comes alive."

Bridget nodded, and a slight smile curved her lips. "'Tis true. Ye're taller and broader than other lasses. Ye've always been. The last time I didn't have to crane my neck back to see ye, I think ye were ten," Bridget said as she stood on her tiptoes and reached up to tuck a wayward black curl behind Nellore's ear. "But then, I am small, even for a woman."

Nellore closed her hand around Bridget's and placed a kiss on her knuckles. "We are a funny pair. Are we not?" Then she pressed her lady's tiny hand against her own heartbeat as her words spilled out with a fervor she could no longer contain.

"There is valor inside of me. I want to fight. I am not afraid to die. Death comes to us all. 'Tis inescapable. If I must die, I would rather do so fighting for my family, for freedom. My da and Logan and Garik do not fight because they are men. If that were true, then all men would be warriors, but they are not. Some are not suited for battle while others are cowards. MacKinnon warriors follow Angus Og and our king because they have defiant spirits. Because they will not stay behind and contribute naught when they can go and fight for what is right, and they are willing to die to defend this country and its people from tyranny. This too is my calling, but instead I remain behind. My strength dwindles and so do my skills."

"Nellore, I ken ye train before first light every day just as ye did with Logan as a child. For five years now, the men have been gone, and in all that time, I doubt ye've lived a single day without climbing a cliff wall or swinging your sword."

"But I am seventeen. I ken now what in youth is impossible to know—futility. As a child I clung to my dreams, yearning for what I know now to be impossible. 'Tis folly to keep pouring my soul into the hopes of one day being a warrior, but what terrifies me more than anything else is complacency. Now that I am a woman, I have striven to put aside my warrior's heart, but alas, I find without that dream my heart is empty." A sad smile curved her lips as she continued. "I feel like a fool."

"Your heart will be full once more," Bridget said. "Never forget that in my youth I was an outcast. The clan that loves me this day, feared and hated me. My life was defined by isolation and anger." Her tone changed and a warmth entered her eyes. "And now I am the lady of this clan, beloved by all." She gave Nellore a wry smile. "Stranger things than ye finding fulfillment have happened, my dear."

Nellore nodded as she stared at the ground.

"Need I remind ye that your story is already touched by magic. I found ye abandoned on the moors only days old, and against all odds ye survived."

Nellore nodded once more but still did not look up. She had often listened to Bridget recount the tale of how she had been found, nearly dead and alone as a babe on the moors. At the time, Brenna had been childless, unable to conceive—or so everyone had thought. Nellore became the babe Brenna had prayed for, and then not three years later Brenna was blessed with another child. Only Rose had grown in Brenna's womb and not upon the moors.

Bridget continued with her tale. "I picked up your tiny body and touched a kiss to your forehead and was struck by a vision. In my ears thundered the battle cry of this clan, and I saw the badge of the MacKinnon, a Scottish pine, burst into flames. I knew then what I still believe to this day. Your fate and the fate of our clan are somehow crossed. A time will come when you must raise your sword and your valor will be tested. Hold tight to your purpose and courage lest you defy your destiny and find yourself ill-prepared."

"I have the skill and the strength," Nellore said with conviction. "Even Garik commended my ability with a sword."

Bridget grew quiet and eyed her for several moments. Then she appeared to give her attention over to the belt at her tunic as she said absently. "Ye seem to remember Garik fondly enough. Ye speak of him almost as much as your da and Logan."

A flash of surprise coursed through Nellore. Then she sighed and smiled down at Bridget. "Ye can cease the appearance of casual observance," she said. Bridget dropped the ends of her belt as a mischievous smile spread across her face.

"Ye see too much with those silver eyes," Nellore said.

"Then ye admit it. Ye're fond of our young Viking," Bridget said.

"I truly do not ken, Bridget. I suppose Garik does come often to mind, but 'twas five long years since I last saw him. No doubt he has forgotten all about the dirty, feckless lass that I was."

"Ye're not dirty anymore. Perhaps, occasionally a wee bit feckless, but then aren't we all," she said with a wink. "Wait until he sees ye now. Look at how fine and lovely ye've grown," Bridget said.

"Nay. I am neither fine nor lovely, but grown I have—too much in fact," she said with a sigh as she stared out to sea once more. Longing still ate at her heart. "I do think of Garik, and so what does that mean? I will tell ye what it means. It means I've traded one impossible dream for another."

"Why should thoughts of Garik seem beyond the realm of possibility?" Bridget asked.

"The last time I saw him I was twelve and holding a sword to a man's neck—not the sort of behavior a man looks for in a wife. He is also not of Mull. Doubtless, when our men are at last released from battle, he will journey home to the Orkney Islands. Chances are I will never see Garik again."

"Well, ye seem to have worked out the mysteries of fate for yourself, and here I thought the future was unknown," Bridget said, dryly.

"I am simply trying to be realistic. I care not to lose myself once again to childish whimsies."

"And I am simply reminding ye that stranger things have happened," Bridget said with a knowing smile.

Nellore watched the surf rise and crash against unyielding rocks. "I can see them now, brandishing their swords, charging into battle atop fine steeds," she said with a sigh. "If only it were me, Bridget. If only it were me."

Chapter Six

Nellore stood at the end of the dock at the small port of Gribun. Anticipation coursed through her. She felt overwhelmed with joy as a ship in the distance drew closer.

"Can ye see anyone yet?" Rose asked as she squinted her eyes. Like Rose, Nellore was straining to make out the figures moving about the deck. A few men lumbered between those rowing to reach for the sail, which they in turn began to pull down.

"I see Da," Rose shouted, her sky-blue eyes alight with joy. "And Logan. Oh, Nellore, they're coming home. Da is coming home." Rose flung her arms around Nellore's waist.

Nellore squeezed her sister's petite frame as she stared at the one man on board not clad in the MacKinnon plaid. A black leather jerkin and black trousers set him apart, allowing her to fixate on his every move. Even from the distance she could see his black hair and white skin.

"Oh, saints above," she whispered. "'Tis Garik."

"What did ye say?" Rose asked.

"Nothing," she said, peering down into Rose's expectant eyes. "Now, off ye go. Tell our mother that Da's ship approaches."

Rose's smile vanished. Nellore knew it was because Rose assumed she would have to race the distance to their home, which was situated beyond the outskirts of Gribun.

"But it will take me so long. I will miss their arrival," Rose said.

"Wheesht, Rose. Mum is at the keep with Lady Bridget. Hurry now," she said, using a stern voice to urge her sister into a run.

Nellore turned back to watch the approaching ship. Her heart pounded as it drew alongside the dock.

Her father, Duncan, was the first to leap from the railing. He called out her name and rushed to her side.

"Nellore," Duncan said again as he pulled her close. She laughed and squeezed him as hard as she could. "Too tight," Duncan said, pretending he could not breathe.

Then another pair of arms enclosed them both, and she squealed with delight when she smiled up into Logan's bright, silver eyes. "Welcome home," she said.

"Get off, ye big lout," Duncan said to Logan. "I wish to see my girl." Logan pressed a hard kiss to her cheek. Then he backed away. Duncan smiled down at her.

"Ye've become a woman in my absence," he said. "A beautiful and tall woman." Surprise colored his voice as his eyes swept from her toes back to her smiling face. "Ye aren't that much shorter than me now, love."

Logan chimed in behind them. "Aye, I cannot tease ye and call ye my little sister, for there is nothing little about ye now."

"I'm a sight I know," she said as she blushed.

"A grand sight," a deep voice said behind her.

She spun around and found herself staring into Garik's wintry blue eyes.

"Hello again," he said. He was changed and yet exquisitely familiar.

"Hello, Garik," she said.

A slow smile spread across his face, causing her breath to catch. His eyes gleamed like stars.

"Ye're changed," she said softly.

Five summers had passed since last she saw Garik MacKinnon. Then he had been a young man with only seventeen years to his credit. Now at two and twenty, he had lost the remnants of the boy. Before her stood a formidable man. His black leather jerkin fitted across his broad chest. His wavy black hair had grown and now gleamed beneath the sun, falling past his shoulders. She thought he never appeared more handsome. He was strong, fierce and mesmerizing.

"Where is the wee lass, I remember?" he said. "Before me stands a woman." His eyes searched hers and then traveled the length of her tall frame. She recognized the glimmer of appreciation in his eyes. She dipped her head to conceal the blush that warmed her cheeks, but then she regretted the loss of his gaze. Her eyes found his once more. She stood straight and tall. She would not hide from him.

He took a step forward. His closeness thrilled and terrified her all at once. She stopped breathing as she watched his hand reach out and then his fingers grazed her cheek. He smelled of the sun and the sea, of faraway lands and adventure. Her chest tightened against the desire his touch inflamed. The wind picked up and whipped her hair into a frenzy. She closed her eyes and laughed as the strands covered her face.

"You have vanished," he said, his voice deep and unhurried. The allure of his strange accent washed over her. He brushed the hair from her eyes, then withdrew a strip of leather from a satchel that hung across his chest. Circling her, he stood at her back, gathering her thick mane in his hand. While he fought the wind to contain her hair, his fingers brushed her neck and throat, sending a rush of sensation down her spine. When he set about tying the leather, he drew closer, and she could feel the heat of his body behind her. Her heart raced. She breathed in his smell. His heat and scent surrounded her. She felt as though she were under siege, but never had an assault been more welcome. And then his hand gripped her waist. The touch was fleeting. Just as suddenly, he was gone, but the pressure of his hand remained.

For a moment, she did not know herself. Her hands hung useless at her side. Her eyes fixated on the choppy water, and she listened intently to the ship rapping against the side of the dock.

"Nellore," a voice called, breaking through the haze of her thoughts.

Her mother and father were standing arm and arm and looking at her expectantly.

"Aye, mum," she answered.

"I do not trust ye by the docks alone," Brenna said as she wrapped her arm around Duncan's waist. "Ye're liable to sail off in search of trouble."

Logan walked over to her and took her hand in his. "Good and calloused," he said as he examined her palm. "Ye've continued your training."

"I swear if ye start encouraging the lass again, Logan, I will beat the life out of ye. Do ye ken?" Duncan said. His tone held a warning his smile could not hide.

"'Tis too late for that," Logan said, clearly undeterred. "I'd wager these hands have gripped a sword every day since we left. And besides, look at the lass. She's as tall as any warrior."

"She is that," Garik said. Her heart raced. She could feel his eyes on her body. They burned where they touched as though his hands caressed her skin. Her eyes left his, and she suddenly was very aware that everyone stared at her, except for Rose. She looked to Logan. Embarrassed, thinking they had all read her mind, she cleared her throat and joined her mum and da. Pressing a kiss to Duncan's cheek she said, "I've missed ye so much, Da." Duncan pulled Nellore and Brenna close. Then he reached past Logan and grabbed Rose, also pulling her to his chest. His black eyes gleamed. "I've missed all my bonny lasses," he said.

They walked together toward the village, meeting kinfolk along the way. Joyful word of the warriors' return had spread throughout the village. Anna, Bridget's daughter, rushed past them without a word, her eyes and heart intent on her husband, Cormac, who still lingered on the docks. Nellore joined the merriment, but as they strode along, she was ever aware of Garik behind her. Despite how she longed to, she dared not look back for fear the feeling he had stirred within her might be revealed in her eyes. She blushed again as her hand touched her waist. It still burned from the pressure of his hand.

AS GARIK WALKED TOWARD the village with Logan, they were joined by their laird. Five years had gone by and he could see the passing of time etched across Ronan's face. His stride had slowed somewhat, but Garik was pleased to note that his wits were as sharp as ever. In that moment, his mind drifted home to the Orkney Islands and he wondered after the well-being of his own grandfather, Aidan. He hoped Aidan and the rest of his family fared as well. Why he had not gone home to the Orkney Islands when the Bruce gave them leave, he could not say for sure—only that somehow, he had felt compelled to Mull. And then his eyes settled once more on the tall, black-haired lass walking in front of him.

He had not been prepared for Nellore. The last time he saw her, she had been a child, but she was a child no longer. She had fulfilled every promise of womanhood and then some. She walked beside her father, her head barely below his. On her other side, walked her mother, Brenna, who was a beautiful woman with her shoulder length red curls, but Nellore soared above her in height. From behind, it gave the impression that Nellore was the mother and Brenna the daughter.

His eyes traveled from her broad shoulders to her firm waist, the waist his hand had been unable to resist touching. His eyes dropped lower, following the gentle curve of her hips, which swayed with captivating power and grace. Never, in all his travels, had he seen a woman like her. She transcended beauty. She was the embodiment of splendor. Everything about her, from her hair to her eyes to her strong hands, challenged him, enticed him. He had known she would grow into a captivating woman, but her allure defied all reason.

He half-listened to Ronan as he spoke of new trouble with the MacLeans. Apparently, their unruly neighbors to the south continued to cross their border bent on thievery and destruction, although it would seem they had grown bolder. Their typical harassment of the cottars on the outskirts of Gribun had moved inland. Last month, Ronan reported they had even broken into the stores near the Ledaig House, which Ronan had had to explain was a newly constructed, long, thatched hall near the stores they had built especially for weddings and other festivities.

"They've not dared tinker with our stores for decades," Ronan said. "The MacLean is old and bedridden. I believe his sons vie for power. The eldest, Balfour, has some sense, but he is as greedy as any MacLean. The younger brothers are as dumb as fence posts and wicked in spirit. I'm sorry, lads," Ronan said. "Ye've been given a short leave from war only to come home to more conflict."

"Do not fash yourself, grandfather," Logan said. "We wouldn't want to return to the Bruce lazy and fat, would we?"

"We will help you set things right before we are gone," Garik promised.

"'Tis glad I am ye're home but there is much to be done," Ronan said. "The summer will go swiftly by."

Garik's gaze once more followed the sway of Nellore's hips. "Aye," he murmured, "there is much to be done."

Chapter Seven

Nellore's hut sat in exquisite isolation, east of the village, beyond rolling moorland, at the foot of a steep hill. To the north they could see the firth of Lorn. When a storm swept through, the waves would crash against the rock-strewn shore. The east side of the land ran alongside a narrow but swift river that wound into a nearby forest. Wildflowers covered the slopes and fields. Many believed it was the finest stretch of earth on Mull. When Duncan was away at war, the land was always included in the nightly watch to safeguard Brenna, Rose, and Nellore. Although Brenna was the first to say it was Nellore that truly safeguarded their lives when the men were absent.

Duncan had left before first light to meet Ronan and Logan. The men intended to make the rounds, visiting the crofters strewn across northern Mull, checking on the security of their borders and collecting the rents; whereas the ladies had set out together at dawn to head into the village. Brenna and Rose wished to visit Anna while Nellore volunteered to purchase what they needed for supplies. She had been happy to volunteer when she had learned Garik had not joined the men on their rounds.

She ducked her head into the blacksmith's stall with several pairs of shears, which needed repair before they could harvest the season's wool. While she waited, she could not help but peek out every now and then to scan the village for Garik. Her mind still reeled from their last exchange. Her attraction to him had been instantaneous and powerful, and she had no wish to deny it. She remembered the feel of the fleeting squeeze of his hand at her waist. Each time her mind returned to that moment, heat rushed to her cheeks. The sound of his lilting voice echoed in her mind. He possessed a strange allure she had no intention of resisting.

As she waited for the smithy to finish with their tools, she leaned against a wooden post and eyed the passersby, always on the lookout for black hair and wintry blue eyes. It was then that she spied her good friend, Mary.

"Mary," she called. With a promise to collect the tools before her return home, she raced from the stall. As she drew nearer to her friend, a little bundle with a shocking mop of red curls hurled herself into Nellore's arms.

"Oh, my sweet lass," Nellore squealed as she pressed kisses to the giggling girl's cheeks. Then she leaned over and kissed Mary too. "I cannot believe our good fortune," Nellore began. "'Tis rare that we both come to the village at the same hour." Then she paused as she studied her friend's face. The telltale signs of worry were visible in her drawn skin and unkempt, red hair. Typically, fastidious about her appearance, Nellore was also surprised to note Mary's wrinkled and stained tunic.

"Are ye not well?" Nellore asked.

"I am fat," she said with a slight smile. "But otherwise, I am well."

Nellore pressed a hand to Mary's swollen stomach. She guessed Mary did not have long to wait for her third babe to make its way into the world. She once again met Mary's troubled gaze. "Something weighs on ye. I know it."

Mary nodded her head and she sighed. "Aye," she said. "'Tis my Gordon. He has been suffering from terrible stomach bouts. I've stuffed him full of cabbage and mint broth but to no avail." The next instant Mary's expression lightened somewhat as she held out her basket. She pulled the cloth from the top, revealing several small vials stopped with wax. "I've hope," she said. "I have just come from the keep. Bridget has given me a syrup made with horehound and laurel. She swore to me that it would relieve his trouble."

Nellore smiled encouragingly. "Ah, now, ye see. He should be feeling better in no time. Ye know as well as I that there is no finer healer than our lady," she said.

"That is a truth if ever I've heard one. We always include Bridget in our daily prayers. What this clan would do without her I dread to imagine."

"We are lucky, indeed," Nellore said. The little lass in her arms continued to squeeze her neck. "Oh, I've missed ye too, Maggie."

Nellore felt a light tap on her shoulder. She turned around and her breath hitched as she found herself staring into Garik's ice blue eyes.

"Garik," she said, smiling as she continued to stare up at him, but then she noticed his own smile did not quite reach his eyes, causing hers to falter. "Good morrow," she said nervously.

His attention turned to Maggie. He tipped his knuckle playfully under Maggie's chin. "I am glad to see you, Nellore," he said. "Your child is beautiful."

She could not suppress the chuckle that rose in her throat. "Nay, this is Mary's daughter. I've yet to marry—I...I mean I have no children," she stammered.

A brilliant smile suddenly lit his face. "Good," he said quickly.

All the world seemed to slip away except for the large half Viking standing before her, but then a throat cleared, breaking the silence. She knew it was Mary's polite way of pointing out that Nellore was standing in the midst of a busy village path staring at a man with her mouth agape like a simpleton or a woman smitten. Dear God above, she had to think of something to say. She cleared her own throat then and motioned to Mary.

"Garik, have ye had the pleasure of meeting Mary?" Nellore asked.

"Aye, some years ago during the Yule celebration and, actually, several other occasions," he said smoothly. "What brings ye to town, Mary?"

"My husband, Gordon, is not well. I came to see Bridget about the matter."

"Please accept my sympathy. I remember Gordon well from my youth. He was a strong lad who I'm sure has grown into a strong man. He will surely be better in no time," he said. He drew closer and tugged lightly on Maggie's red curls. "Now, I do not believe I've had the pleasure of meeting this little lass," he said.

Nellore turned so that Garik could see Maggie better. "Maggie, love, this is Garik," she said.

Maggie turned away, nestling her face in the crook of Nellore's neck while clinging tighter to her rag baby. Nellore laughed and smiled at Garik. "She is shy, and she never puts down Bridget."

"Bridget?" Garik asked.

Nellore chuckled. "She named her rag baby after our lady."

Garik put his fingers to his lips, signaling for Nellore and Mary to keep quiet. Then he touched Maggie's shoulder. She lifted her head and looked to where Garik had stood, but he had already ducked out of sight behind Nellore. A moment passed and then he peeked over Nellore's shoulder. The wee lass erupted into giggles as Garik continued his game. After a few more rounds, Garik reached his arms out to her. She did not hesitate this time as she strained to leave Nellore's embrace for Garik's. Nellore could not blame her as she herself looked longingly at his strong arms.

Mary laughed alongside Nellore. "Thank ye, both of ye," she said. "Ye've lifted my spirits. Laughter has been in low supply around our home these last weeks. But with that in mind, home is really where I ought to be heading. We've a ways to go yet."

"Do you still live in the valley?" he asked.

"Aye," she said. "But 'tis not really so far."

"I would argue differently for someone in your condition. Wait here. I will return at once." Then he turned on his heel and headed toward the stables.

Mary raised a questioning brow at Nellore.

"I do not ken," Nellore said.

"Ye don't suppose he is off to the stables and will return with a horse I am meant to climb onto?" she said.

Nellore laughed as she stared after her Scottish Viking. "I'm not certain what he is up to, but I assure ye, he will do no such thing."

"Nellore!" Mary exclaimed as a saucy glint filled her eyes. "I saw that."

"Ye saw what?" she said as she busied herself dusting off Maggie's tunic.

"I saw that smile."

"What smile? I do not ken what ye're talking about," she said as she fought to suppress the very smile which Mary had accused her of flashing.

"Ah-ha!" Mary said, laughing. "Ye cannot hide that look from me. Ye fancy him. Don't ye?"

At that moment, Garik came around the corner driving a wagon. "Here he comes. Enough of this talk," Nellore said. The fluttering of her heart quickened the closer he drew.

"At long last, a man has stolen your heart."

"Wheest," Nellore said as she turned pleading eyes to her friend.

"I won't say a word," Mary said. "I won't have to. Your eyes will do all the talking."

"Wheest, Mary. I beg ye." She took a few deep breaths, hoping to rid her face of the blush her friend's words had brought to her cheeks.

Garik pulled beside them with the wagon. The sun glinted off his long, black hair. She admired how his black leather jerkin strained to cover the wide breadth of his shoulders.

"Shall I take you home in comfort?" he asked Mary.

The musical way he spoke struck Nellore to the core. God above, he was a gorgeous man.

He swept his hand out, ushering their gazes to behold the bed of the carriage. The rough-hewn wood lay hidden beneath a thick blanket.

Mary smiled as she greedily eyed the wagon bed. "'Tis good of ye. This is one kindness I am happy to accept."

As Mary strode past Nellore she whispered, "I saw ye drinking your fill when he pulled up just now." Nellore blushed and urged her friend to be silent.

Garik hopped down and offered a hand to Mary. With a sigh, she settled herself on the blanket. Once situated, she reached out for Maggie and the two snuggled down together. Nellore smiled at her contented-looking friend, knowing it was likely the first time Mary had been off her feet all day. Five years her senior, Mary had wed her childhood sweetheart at the tender age of fifteen. Both she and Gordon were children of cottars and had grown up together in the valley. Now they had two children and another on the way and a home filled with warmth and happiness and plenty of noise—at least when they all enjoyed good health. Nellore worried over Gordon's condition and dreaded to think of Mary's heartbreak if he did not recover.

A shadow suddenly fell upon the resting mother and child, and she knew Garik stood behind her. With a deep breath, she turned. She had to tilt her head back to meet his gaze, which thrilled her to no end.

"Ye're very tall." For pity's sake, had she actually said that out loud?

A smile tugged at his lips. "So are you," he said softly.

"I suppose ye should be getting Mary home," she said.

He nodded. "Would you join me for the ride?"

A nervous knot lodged in her throat, making it impossible for her to accept his invitation, but just as she was working up the courage to tell him that she would love nothing more a voice called out her name. She turned to find her mother waving her over. "'Tis time to return home," Brenna said.

She turned back to face him. "I have to go," she said before stepping away, but he grabbed her arm and whirled her back to face. She waited for him to speak, but he said nothing. He only smiled while his gaze passed over her entirety with slow deliberation. His hand then loosened and slowly traveled the length of her arm all the way down until just their fingertips touched and then like a whisper his touch was gone, yet her heart still pounded with yearning.

Chapter Eight

With a mortar and pestle, Nellore mashed a heap of blaeberries that would be added to the batch of blue dye Brenna stirred over the pit fire. They labored in preparation for the sheep shearing that would commence in the morning. Nellore tried to keep her mind on the task at hand, but images of Garik crept into her thoughts, and suddenly her hands ceased mashing while fantasy took over.

"Nellore, lass," Brenna said as she reached up to stroke her fingers down Nellore's cheek. "What am I to do with ye? Ye were daydreaming. Tell me ye weren't dreaming of heading off to battle again."

"Nay, mum," she said, flashing Brenna a smile. "Ye ken I've put that fancy to rest."

Brenna wrapped her arms around her daughter. "Your valor does not go to waste. 'Tis used each day that ye care for this family and your clan."

She nodded, beaming down at her mother, and pressed a kiss to her cheek. "I love ye, mum," she said.

"And I love ye. Oh my, but ye're all smiles and daydreams today," Brenna said, shaking her head. "Off with ye, lass. Go stretch your legs. We'll need more blaeberries before long. Just bring your sword so I don't worry after ye."

Nellore set out with a basket on her arm and a skip in her step. The sun warmed her skin. Everywhere she turned the earth shone with the promise of vitality. She headed through the wood, which bordered the eastern orchards.

A broad expanse of apple trees surrounded her. The limbs shimmered with pink blossoms. As the wind blew, the air became thick with drifting petals. She spun around and around while she raised her face to the sky. The petals caressed her skin on their way to their earthly bed. Then she heard the snap of a branch behind her, and she whirled around but nothing seemed amiss. She held her breath as she listened. In a different direction than the first disturbance, she heard another branch snap. She whirled around again. This time she saw a shadow flit between two trees. She withdrew her blade from behind her back and eased toward the noise.

Suddenly, she was snatched from behind and thrust against a hard chest. Fear shot through her as lips brushed her ear and the heat of her captor's warm breath caressed her neck. She shook her head, clearing away her surprise while her courage sprang to the fore. She threw her head back, producing a satisfying crunch as her skull connected with something much softer. A loud curse rang out and the grip on her arms loosened. She spun around and pushed the man to the ground, thrusting her blade beneath his neck.

"Garik," she exclaimed. "Och, Garik! I'm so sorry. I did not realize it was ye."

He held his forearm to his bleeding nose. She knelt to the ground and swept up the end of her tunic, gathering it into a bundle. "Allow me," she said. He pulled his hand away, and the blood raced down his mouth and chin. "Oh, God, Garik, for-give me," she said as she pressed the fabric to his nose.

He chuckled. "I should have known better than to sneak up on you," he said. "Do not fret so. It is nothing."

"Do not speak until the bleeding stops," she said.

His sheer blue eyes locked with hers as she continued to hold her tunic to his nose. They were so close, he sitting and she on her knees. The hand that did not hold the compress cradled his head, her fingers laced through his black hair. She could smell him and feel the heat of his body. Her breathing quick-ened as his unwavering gaze held hers. She blushed under his scrutiny.

"I'm going to check whether the bleeding has lessened," she said, pulling the fabric away. "It appears to have stopped." She dabbed at his skin to clean away the stain of blood she had not been quick enough to catch. "I don't think I broke it."

One side of his lips lifted into a lazy sideways smile that told her he would not care if she had. "I am more concerned about your tunic," he said, pointing to the stained, wadded fab-ric still in her hands. She looked down and saw that her knees and the bottom of her thighs were exposed to his gaze. She blushed again and quickly smoothed the fabric in place. His hand grazed her thigh, his touch as soft as a whisper, and yet it burned through the fabric to her skin and then throughout her whole body. "I would do it all again," he said.

A smile came unbidden to her lips as she lost herself in his shining eyes. Strands of long, black hair had escaped from the leather thong he used to secure it back at the nape of his neck. Her eyes then roamed over his broad shoulders. He wore a soft brown leather jerkin and a plain linen shirt beneath it. His trousers were gray, and he wore no shoes on his feet. She turned her gaze back to his face and saw a look of amusement in his eyes. She had been caught staring. She stood up then and dusted off her tunic. He continued to stare up at her and seemed in no hurry to pursue any other endeavor. She passed several thrilling moments under his watch. When at last he stood, she once more savored his height. He did not quite tower over her—no man did that—but he did almost make her feel small. Almost.

"Shall we walk then?" he asked.

She nodded, accepting his arm. "What are you collecting?" he said, motioning toward the basket swinging at her side.

"We begin the shearing on the morrow. My mum sent me to gather more blaeberries," she said. Then she stopped and turned to face him. "I should be asking ye the same question. What brings ye this far east of Gribun?"

"I was heading into the wood to hunt," he said, drawing closer.

Nerves coursed through her. "I shouldn't linger overly long. My mother waits for the berries."

"I will help you then," he said. "But first, you owe me that ride."

A weak protest rose to her lips, but she swallowed it back down, instead allowing him to pull her toward his horse. He ran his hand down his horse's sleek nose.

"What is he named?" she asked.

"Ulf. In my language it means wolf. I named him so because of the white patch on his chest."

"He is beautiful," she said, running her hand across the horse's black side. "He is not unlike ye with your black hair and white skin. Ye even have eyes like a wolf. I've never seen eyes like yours."

She gasped as he came behind her and scooped her into his arms. She clung to his neck and laughed out loud. "Carry me about all day and ye'll not need to train for a fortnight. Ye'll be as strong as an ox."

"This may come as a surprise, my dear, but despite your height and strength you feel like air in my arms." He lifted her onto Ulf's back and pulled himself behind her. "Your hair smells of lavender," he said while he started to undo the bindings of her scabbard. "Do you mind? I had hoped to feel something softer than steel in my arms while we rode."

"I do not mind," she said as she gripped the horse's mane to keep her arms from trembling. He secured her sword to his saddle, and then his arms came around her, pulling her flush against his chest.

Riding west, they galloped across the moors. He loved the feel of her body pressing against his. The curve of her waist demanded his touch, and her soft hair brushed his face, surrounding him with her scent while they raced across the moors. No other woman could feel as good as Nellore. Their bodies fit together as though destined to be joined. The sweet sound of her laughter filled his ears when he urged Ulf to gallop ever faster. Lost as he was in the pleasure of her body pressed against his, he had not observed the shift in scenery. He pulled tight on the reins when he glimpsed the hut of the Witch of Dervaig in the distance.

"What is it?" she asked. "Why have we stopped?" He saw her hand rise to feel for her sword, but her fingers grappled at air.

"I have your sword," he reminded her. "I did not mean to bring us this far west," he said.

She turned in her seat and looked up into his eyes. "Are you afraid?" she asked.

He shrugged. "I'm not afraid. I've never given the legend of the witch much due since I first heard the tales as a lad. In fact, my grandfather, Aidan MacKinnon, told me not to fear the witch, but when I pressed him further, he refused to speak more on the subject."

"If ye're not afraid, then why have we stopped?"

He smiled down at her. "When Angus Og first arrived five years ago, and we set out to fight for our king, your father told me something I will never forget."

"What is that?" she asked.

"He said that trouble finds everyone eventually. You never need go in search of it."

She smiled. Her father had said those same words to her many times. She turned and stared at Bridget's old hut. She had been inside on several occasions over the years. Refusing to let her ancestral home fall into disrepair, Bridget had secreted across the moors with Nellore at her side to clean and maintain the small hut. She loved its fanciful round door. She turned to look at Garik, suddenly filled with longing to tell him the truth: there was no witch, but the words remained trapped by her conscience. It was not her secret to tell.

"We have similar legends on the Orkney Islands," he said while he turned his horse around.

"Do ye now. I would love to hear about your home," she said.

"We have the most fearsome creatures of all, the Finmen. The stories always begin the same way. 'Beware the Finman.' They used to terrify me as a child," he said, chuckling.

"What exactly is a Finman?" she asked.

"Finmen are magical creatures, not unlike men in appearance, although much stronger and taller with hollow eyes and sorrowful auras. They sail in phantom boats that require no oar or sail. They compel their vessels forward with their minds. And sorry is the fisherman who unknowingly drifts into Finmen waters."

"What torment does the Finman make?" she asked.

"He wreaks havoc on human ships. Chances are he will send the fisherman barreling toward jagged rocks or into an approaching storm. Needless to say, the fisherman is unlikely to make shore again."

"A chilling tale, indeed. Are there others?" she asked eagerly.

He laughed, enjoying her delight. "Is there more than one star in the sky?" he said. "Telling stories is what we do best on the Orkney Islands. The winters are much longer with scant daylight. After yule, the sun does not rise until mid-morning and it sinks below the horizon well before the evening meal. That is when we come together and tell stories and play music."

"It sounds grand," she said.

"It is." Then he added softly, "so are you."

Nellore blushed and was quiet for several moments, and then she asked, "Is that how ye view the witch—as a legend like the Finmen?"

"Don't you?" he replied.

"What do ye make of her hut?"

He smiled, "Ah, yes, the witch's hut with the snake fang door. Well, mayhap the hut did once belong to a woman who some believed to be a witch, but for all we know her bones have long since been polished by the birds and sea air, lying at peace on her pallet where she died."

A shudder coursed through her. He had just described Bridget's fate had Ronan not witnessed her rare beauty in the woods on that fateful day long ago. Without Ronan and his love, Bridget would have spent the long years of her life alone.

"You trembled," he said while pulling her closer. "You have not to fear, Nellore. I promise you, the Witch of Dervaig is only the stuff of legend."

"Trust me when I say, Garik, that I do not fear the witch."

They rode on and she listened transfixed while he continued telling tales of the Orkney Islands. He smiled often and spoke fondly of his family.

"Why did ye not go home? When the king gave ye leave, that is. Why come back to Mull?" she asked.

"I could not have told you when we first set out on our return only that I felt compelled." Then he reached out and stroked her cheek. "Though now I understand."

She turned away as pink once more colored her cheeks, but then she turned back to face him and held his gaze. He loved her display of both candor and innocence. He lost himself in the majesty of her green eyes.

"We should be heading back," she said. "I still have berries to pick, and ye've nothing to show for your hunt."

"I wouldn't say that," he said, smiling as he tightened his hold on her waist. "I've a confession to make, Nellore. I was not hunting. I followed you."

"You followed *me*? But why?"

"I saw you crossing the moors, and I could not tear my eyes away, but you kept on walking, and because I still wished to see you, I followed."

"Oh," she said, looking away, but then she turned and looked him square in the eye. "I'm glad ye did."

He took her hand and pressed a kiss to her palm. "I will take you home."

She rested against his chest as they rode toward Gribun. When they neared the outskirts of the village. She asked him to stop. "Leave me here," she said.

"But your home is still some distance away."

"Aye, but I would rather not return home with an empty basket."

"Do you think your parents would object to the company?"

"Nay—not to the company but to my being alone with the company."

"Then I need to pay a visit to your home. Do I not?"

The sun had never shown as bright as Nellore's smile. "See that ye do," she said, before hurrying away.

Chapter Nine

Nellore rose before first light just as she did every morning and met Hamish outside her croft to train. The old warrior had taught her many things over the years, honing not just her skill with a blade but also her instincts as a warrior. "Ye must be able to guess the enemy's next move. Ye must know it even before he does," Hamish had often said.

When the sun fully emerged from beneath the horizon, she bid Hamish farewell and turned to go back inside her hut, but her step faltered when she saw her father leaning against the doorframe, watching her. His eyes beamed with pride.

"Ye've truly grown into a remarkable woman," he said.

"Ye don't mind," she said, lifting her sword.

"Nay, I don't mind so long as ye don't go looking for trouble like ye did as a lass."

Sheathing her sword, she fell into his arms and breathed in his scent. An immediate sense of security surrounded her. "I'm so glad your home, Da."

"Me too, my wee lass who is not so wee anymore," he said with a grin. "Me too."

Together they went inside. Brenna and Rose still slumbered.

"Shall we let them sleep?" Duncan asked. "Today will be a long day."

"Let mum rest a while longer, but I promised Rose I would wake her early. She wanted to visit Mary and Gordon before we started with the sheep."

She watched as her da's eyes settled first on Rose and then on Brenna. His lips curved into a smile as he quietly returned to the pallet he shared with Brenna. "I will enjoy a lazy morning with my wife then," he whispered. "Wake your sister and hurry on your way." With a wink he nestled under the covers beside Brenna. Brenna stirred a little and sighed when his arms came around her. Nellore smiled at her parents. Their love for each other was as constant as the love they bore their children. She could only hope she would be as lucky in love as her parents. Her thoughts brought images of Garik to the fore of her mind. She closed her eyes and felt the grip of his arms around her waist as they galloped over the moors.

"On with ye, lass," Duncan said, pulling her from her daydream. "I would have some time alone with my wife this morn."

She smiled and rushed to Rose's side. She shook Rose awake but pressed a finger to her lips to signal that she must remain quiet. Rose sat up and smiled when Duncan shooed them with a gesture toward the door. Splashing a little water on her face, Rose then turned and grabbed some twigs and mint to chew on their journey to the valley.

Nellore and Rose giggled quietly when they eased the door shut on their parents. Then they rushed to the stables and saddled their horses. The sun had just begun its ascent when they set out for the valley to check on Gordon's progress.

They skirted around Gribun to hasten their journey, knowing they had a long and arduous day ahead of them. The shearing was a favorite time for Nellore, but it was very hard work.

If they traveled through the village, they would be stopped by friends who would want to exchange news, and they simply could not afford the time. Once beyond the boundaries of the village proper, they urged their mounts into a gallop and set out over the open moors.

Nellore's horse sensed the danger before she did. He slowed to a trot and refused to comply with her commands to hasten forward.

"Those are strange clouds," Rose said as she pointed to gray streaks mingling with the morning mist and the golden sky in the distance.

Nellore covered her eyes against the rising sun as she studied the unusual sky. Then the wind shifted, and an acrid scent invaded her nostrils. "Those aren't clouds. 'Tis smoke." She kicked her mount hard in the flanks, and at last the beast complied. As they hastened to the top of the nearest hill, she was given a view of the distant valley, which appeared to have been swallowed by fire.

"Quickly, Rose, bring your horse around."

"Should we not carry on and help them," Rose asked, her face pale with terror.

"Nay, we must sound the alarm."

They raced back the way they had come, only this time they rode straight into the village, stirring dust and skirting livestock as they sped into the courtyard of Dun Ara Castle.

"The valley is aflame," Nellore cried as she slid from her horse. "The alarm, Thomas," she shouted to a lad who stared up at her with a dumbstruck expression. At her command he raced off toward the tower where the bell waited to be struck so that it might sing out to the crofters who were the most vulnerable to attack. The gates to the keep opened, releasing a torrent of warriors. She glimpsed Garik among their number. The stable teemed with chaos while several young lads raced about to carry out the stable master's commands. When readied, warriors seized the horses, swinging themselves in place and galloping off toward the smoke, which could now be seen billowing against the brightening sky.

The singed smell reached her nostrils. "Rose, get ye home," she called out to her sister who stood amid the confusion with a sickly look upon her face. Then Nellore mounted her horse and hastened back toward the fire.

The thunder of hooves tore up the earth as the mighty force of the MacKinnons fought to outrun the Highland wind that would feed the flames and spread the fire. The charred valley stretched out before her.

"Thanks be to Mary and all the angels," Nellore cried when she saw Mary's croft untouched by flame, but others were not as blessed. Several thatch and peat huts had crumbled, engulfed by fire. Towers of smoke stretched toward the sky. The families could do naught but watch their homes fade into ash.

"Maggie," a voice screamed.

Nellore's heart seized in her chest. "Mary?" she shouted. She slid from her horse and rushed about calling to her friend. Then she saw her. Horror gripped Mary's face. "My Maggie," she cried, her mouth wide as a sob rose to her lips.

"Mary," Nellore called as she raced through a barley field that had been spared by the flames, but before she could make it to the other side, strong hands grabbed her, lifting her into the air and astride a familiar black horse.

"Garik," she said. "Put me down. I must get to Mary."

He kicked his horse and charged across the field to Mary's side. With Nellore cradled in his arms, he slid from his mount. "Stay out of the fields," he said. "If a spark lands on the plants and the wind picks up, it might be engulfed before you find a way out."

She nodded, realizing her mistake. "I will be careful," she promised and then turned away, rushing to Mary's side. "Mary," she cried.

"My Maggie," Mary sobbed. "I cannot find her. I've searched everywhere. Oh, please, dear God above, where is she?"

Nellore grabbed Mary's shoulders. Pain twisted her features. "Mary, look at me. Where did ye last see her?"

Mary shook her head, heart-wrenching sobs wracked her shoulders. "I do not ken. She was playing with the other children when the fires began." She fell to her knees. "My Maggie," she sobbed.

Nellore pulled Mary into her arms, "We'll find her," she swore. Then she rose. "I promise ye, Mary. Now, stay where ye are," she said before she turned in search of Garik.

GARIK REACHED DOWN and lifted an old cottar to his feet. Wizened fingers clung to a pitchfork.

"The old codger used to it to fend off the enemy," a cottar named William said as hurried over to help Garik.

The ancient man's white hair was streaked with soot, and tears marred the black stains on his face. "There were too many," he said, turning dazed eyes on Garik. "There was naught we could do."

"You fought valiantly," Garik said as he gently pried the pitchfork from the old man's hands. He then heard his name being shouted. Recognizing Nellore's voice, he scanned his surroundings, but he could not find her through the undulating smoke.

"See to this man," he said to William. Then he stood and shouted, "Nellore."

She raced into his arms. Her chest heaved, and her eyes stretched wide with panic. "Maggie," she gritted, choking back tears.

"What about Maggie?" he said. Then his heart dropped to the pit of his stomach. He grabbed her by the arms. "Is she hurt, Nellore? Speak to me," he said.

She took a deep breath. "I do not ken," she said. "She's missing. Mary said she searched everywhere for her. She is out of her mind with grief." Then she pressed her face into his chest. "So am I," she whispered, but her weakness lasted only a moment. She drew away and squared her shoulders. Her vulnerability disappeared, replaced by fierce determination.

"Gather the men. Find her," she said before turning on her heel.

"Where are *you* going?" he called after her.

"To find Bridget. She will know what to do," she shouted before disappearing once more into the chaos.

Maggie's red curls and pouty lips came to the fore of Garik's mind. "MacKinnons," he shouted. "To me."

A band of warriors soon gathered around him.

"The wee lass, Maggie, has gone missing," he said. He sent three of the men to scour the forest, and then another three to search the fields. "Tread carefully. Watch for signs of fire. If the flames rekindle, you may find yourselves trapped."

As the men departed, Garik turned to find Logan standing behind him. His furrowed brow framed grief-stricken silver eyes. "What do you make of the damage?" Garik asked.

"The crops are burnt. Twenty head of sheep stolen, but these are losses that can be recouped," Logan snarled as his eyes flared with rage, churning their silver depths like molten steel. "But this cannot," he said. Opening his sporran, he removed the remnants of a rag baby. Garik's heart sank to the pit of his stomach. Even with its charred face and scorched body, he recognized it as Maggie's straightaway, and then he remembered Nellore saying that Maggie never put it down.

Fury tore through him as he reached behind his back to seize his blade, but Logan stayed his hand. "Get back, Logan. I will have blood for this."

"If Maggie is dead, we will have our vengeance, but right now we must continue the search. There is still hope," Logan said, although his tone lacked conviction. "Gather the other men and fan out. We must search every croft, every barn, and beneath every bush. She could be out there but still too afraid to come forward."

"God help the MacLean if she is not found, because I will send his black soul straight to hell," Garik growled before storming off through the smoking fields.

For hours, they searched. Just as Logan had instructed, every croft, loft, and hay pile were picked through—any place a lass of three years could fit. Then a sob rent the air. Garik jumped from the loft he was searching and raced outside toward the cries. The scene he glimpsed laid bare his heart. Logan held Maggie's rag baby out for both Mary and Gordon to see. Mary collapsed to her knees, her arms hanging limply at her side and her mouth stretched open to the sky, and from her lips came forth a cry of such agony and loss that it forced the breath from Garik's body. Each gut-wrenching sob cut like a knife twisting into his heart. Gordon stood beside his wife, his face white with shock and his arms outstretched and empty.

Suddenly, another commotion swept through the smoldering fields. Garik ran toward the noise and skidded to a halt. From out of the woods strode the Lady Bridget and Nellore and cradled in Nellore's arms was a bundled blanket with flaming red curls peeking out from the top. His heart gripped in terror. Had they found the poor lass's body? His breath caught as a smile stretched wide, filling Nellore's face, and he knew then Maggie lived.

"Maggie," he yelled. Then he turned around and raced back to Mary and Gordon.

"She lives," he shouted when he drew closer. "She is alive."

He fell to his knees and pulled Mary into his arms. Still, she sobbed, her body racked by the force of her grief. He cupped her cheeks in his hands and forced her to meet his gaze.

"Mary," he said, his voice loud and firm as he tried to be heard over the din of terror that filled her mind, making her oblivious to anything but the shocking loss of her precious child. "Mary, your daughter lives."

Pain continued to cloud her eyes. Garik scooped her into his arms and carried her through the ashen fields. Still, she sobbed, beating his leather jerkin with her fist. The moment they came into Maggie's view the wee lass cried out one word—Mama.

Mary jerked toward the sound and beheld her little girl. Her face crumpled once more, but the sobs that tore from her throat were fueled by an unspeakable joy. It was the sound of hope reborn. She flung herself toward her daughter, stumbling in the ash and soot. Maggie wriggled from Nellore's arms and raced toward her mama. When the two met, they collapsed together in an explosion of tears and kisses. Garik had to turn away, the sweet agony too much to bear. He hurried over to where Lady Bridget and Nellore stood together, arm and arm. Tears streamed down their cheeks.

"Where was she?" Garik asked breathlessly. "We've searched everywhere."

Bridget turned her bright silver eyes to meet his. "She was in one of the caves," she replied.

Garik's eyes widened in surprise. "But the shore is more than two miles from here. We never would have considered such a distance. How did you know to look there?" he asked.

Bridget offered no explanation. She merely shrugged and glanced at Nellore, but the glint Garik witnessed in her queer eyes belied her casual display.

"Lady Bridget," Garik began. "There are so many caves. How did ye know which one to search?"

"Come, Garik," Nellore said, drawing him away. "Let us celebrate."

Questions burned for answers. How did Bridget and Nellore know to look in the caves? He glanced back once more at Bridget whose silver gaze bore into his own.

"Garik," Nellore said. He tore his eyes from his lady's and looked to Nellore. She rose on her toes and whispered, "This world is full of wonder." Then she pressed a kiss to his cheek.

The feel of her full lips on his skin eased his mind. "Indeed, it is," he murmured as he breathed in her scent. "You are proof of that."

Chapter Ten

After a fortnight spent rebuilding the valley, Garik joined the MacKinnon warriors on their march to the training fields. It marked their first session with Ronan after their return from battle. Garik mentally rallied his spirit to meet the challenge ahead. A ruthless task master, Ronan led the march that morning. His long, silvery hair hung past his shoulders, and he walked with a determined stride. The fight had not yet left their laird.

Garik looked east and saw the sun rising above Dun Ara Castle. It was time to begin. Ahead of them stretched the training fields, but they were not empty as he would have expected. Telltale black curls whirled around a tall, sleek form as the sun glinted off the tip of a sword that slashed the morning air. A smile stretched across his face.

"She beat us to it, lads," Ronan said with a laugh. His amber eyes crinkled with a warm smile.

"I did not know Nellore was to be joining us today," Garik said.

"She is not," Duncan snapped at Garik. Then his gaze turned back toward his daughter. "She is up well before first light to train. Like us all, her duties begin when the sun rises, but my lass is not one to shirk her real duties. She rises earlier than the rest of us to play at being a warrior." Duncan's tone of displeasure could not mask the slight smile that curved his lips while he watched his daughter.

"Actually, Duncan, your daughter will be joining us today and every day until ye march again under Scotland's banner," Ronan said.

"She will not," Duncan said as he whirled around to challenge his laird.

"My wife and your wife insist Nellore be able to train. After listening to their considerations, I've given my consent."

"And I say she will not. She is my daughter," Duncan growled.

"Aye, that is true, but I am your laird. And I am her laird. On this matter, my word is final." Ronan stepped forward and turned to address his warriors. "Who among ye will argue against Nellore's strength or skill?"

No one stepped forward.

Ronan called Nellore to him and bid her stand before the warriors. "I would not see Nellore's skills wasted at a time when we are at war both here and abroad," he said. "The MacLean denies responsibility for the fires, but we all ken he is a liar. Most of ye have fought these last years alongside Angus Og, but the war for Scotland's independence is far from won. England still holds Stirling and Roxburgh. However, our own borders are weak. But what is the MacKinnon to do? Do we shirk our duty to our king just to safeguard our home against the MacLeans? Nay," Ronan shouted. "Warriors of Mull, ye will take up arms for the Bruce, which means those of us who remain must do all we can to ensure the safety of our village, our stores, and those who cannot fight. Nellore has proven herself since she was a lass. Her valor and skill surpass that of many men."

Duncan stormed forward, bringing his face but a breath from Ronan's. "Ye do not mean for her to march with the Bruce," Duncan snarled. Garik did not doubt that Ronan was one wrong answer away from a beating, laird or not.

"Nay, Duncan," Ronan said. Duncan eased back, raking his hand through his hair.

"Be still, Duncan, and have faith in me," Ronan said. "I do not seek to put her in harm's way, but I would have her ready to protect those who are more vulnerable—your wife, my wife, your other daughter, my daughters, the children. Nellore is not the same as they and ye know it. God's blood, Duncan, ye should be proud to have fathered a shield maiden of Scotland. Now get back into formation," he growled.

Logan stepped forward then and put his hand on Duncan's shoulder. "Our laird is right, Duncan."

Duncan grabbed Logan's hand and twisted it behind his back.

"He does not mean for her to go to fight. Only that she be ready if the fight is brought to her," Logan said, wincing.

Nellore rushed forward and yanked Logan free from her father's grip. "Da, we train our women to hit a mark with an arrow so that they are not left helpless if our warriors should fail. Such times as these demand we all be tested. Ye know my temperament. I am not the foolish little girl who seeks trouble anymore. Ye can trust me not to be reckless, but I will fight for our people if need be."

Duncan pulled her into a fierce embrace. "I worry for ye, lass," he whispered. "Ye should be thinking of marriage and a family, not climbing cliff walls and sword fighting."

She looked up into his black eyes. "I do think of those things," she said. Then her eyes darted toward Garik who was staring straight at her, smiling. Her lips curved in greeting.

"So, is that where your heart lies then?" Duncan said softly, peering down at her.

Her only answer was the blush she knew warmed her cheeks. Then she fell into line behind Ronan.

Although used to the rigors of training, nothing could have prepared her for the next several hours. She had been able to complete most of the drills and was encouraged by the other warriors who generously praised her efforts. The sun shone at its highest when the ladies arrived.

Bridget and Anna carried baskets of fresh bannock still hot from the flames. Rose and Brenna brought flasks of ale and dried herring. Famished, Nellore sat down beside her da and took a bite of bannock.

"So 'tis Garik ye admire," Duncan said. "Ye don't need to answer. I saw the way ye looked at him." Then he took a drink of ale. He passed her the flask from which she drank heartily. "I would have thought ye fancied Logan," he said.

She almost spit out the mouthful of ale. "Logan! Da, he is like a brother to me. Just the idea of Logan and me is ridiculous." Then she nodded her head in Logan's direction. "Besides, I think someone else pines for him." Both Nellore and Duncan watched as Rose handed Logan a bannock from her basket. Nellore could not hear what the future laird of the MacKinnon said, but judging by the glint in his silver eyes and the blush that colored Rose's cheeks, something kindled between them.

"So that is how it is," Duncan said.

"Aye, but neither of them will admit it."

"If they have not said anything to ye, then how can ye be so certain?"

"Because I have eyes, as do ye," she said with a smile.

Duncan paused and observed Rose and Logan further. "Aye, they are in love. Och, what am I to do with two daughters in love?" he said as he turned his eyes heavenward.

"The good Lord cannot help us, Duncan," Brenna said as she came to stand above them. Nellore smiled up at her mum. "They are grown, and as much as we might wish them to be wee lassies again, there is naught to do but give them wings." Then Brenna stretched her hand out to Nellore. "Come," she said. "For a fortnight, those sheep have suffered this heat. Now that the valley has been put to rights, 'tis time at last for the shearing."

Chapter Eleven

Garik took in the scope of Nellore's home. Such beauty stirred his soul. In the distance, the waves of the Sound of Mull crashed against the shore. Thick forest stretched to the east, and a stream filled the air with music. He wondered whether she would be willing to leave. Then he smiled, realizing he would be willing to surrender his own home and reside permanently on Mull if that was her wish. Ever since he had returned from war and first stared into the endless depths of her warm green eyes, he had begun to fixate on one dream alone—winning Nellore's heart. To him, nothing else mattered.

He descended the steep slope. Rose, who was stirring the boiling contents of a large pot, waved when she noticed his approach. Duncan and Brenna stood together beside their fields. He had yet to spy Nellore.

"Hello, Garik," Duncan said.

Garik dipped his head in greeting. Brenna smiled and bid him welcome.

"Your crops grow well," Garik said. "Who plowed the fields in your absence?"

"Nellore, of course," Brenna answered.

Duncan grunted in reply.

"It may not please ye, my love," Brenna said, "but it pleased her." Then Brenna turned to Garik. "At times, my husband wishes his daughter was less spirited, but I believe we should not take away her purpose. Anyway," she said as she winked at Garik, "Nellore is not the first woman to plow this field."

"Och, woman," Duncan said. "Can ye not keep silent? Every spring am I to be reminded of that one lapse in judgment?"

"Aye," Brenna said, her blue eyes dancing. "Besides, ye've missed five plants and five harvests while ye've marched with our king. I figure that means ye had it coming. Ye see, Garik," Brenna said as she gave her husband a mischievous grin, "this man once sat about while the summer drifted away, leaving me to tend my fields alone. I had not half the strength of my daughter. Nellore can manage an ox-driven plow. I turned this stretch of earth ye see with only a hand plow. Ye can imagine the bloody mess it made of my hands." Brenna said. Then she thrust her palms out for Garik to examine. "Ye can still see the scars."

Garik chuckled when Brenna scowled at her husband. Duncan grabbed her, pulling her flush against him. "Aye, but I don't recall ye complaining about the careful way I tended your wounds."

The blush that colored Brenna's white cheeks told Garik all he needed to know about what transpired while Duncan had cared for her bloodied hands. Garik smiled and turned away from the loving couple. He decided to go in search of Nellore.

He found her around the backside of the croft, standing beneath a large oak tree. The afternoon sun slanted through the branches, alighting her black hair with streaks of amber fire. Tied onto a post protruding from the earth near the tree was a sheep blinded by its shaggy fleece. Nellore stood with a sharpening stone, smoothing away the dullness from a set of shears. Raking his eyes over her sleek form, he was once again struck by the duality of her grace and strength. She still had not seen him. She ran her thumb over the shears, checking for the right sharpness. Satisfied, she set the stone and shears beside the tethered sheep.

Gathering her hair into her hand, she twisted the length all the way to the bottom and looped it through itself, tying a knot at the nape of her neck. Then she untethered the sheep and laid it on its side. With the animal straddled between her legs, she began cutting through the fleece at the neck, a task generally performed by the men of the clan. Garik never imagined he would envy a sheep of all creatures, but he realized there was, indeed, a first for everything while he stared at the beast's coveted position between Nellore's thighs.

Dear God above, she was magnificent. He could tell how much she loved work that used the strength of her body. She smiled when the sheep bucked slightly and paused to sooth the animal with a gentle touch. From that point on, the sheep lay still, allowing her to navigate the shears from one side to the other. He could not tear his eyes away. After a time, she sat up as the fleece fell away. Then she laughed as she swung her leg off the beast's side, giving it a swat on the rump to encourage it to jump on its way.

It was then that she noticed him. A red flush colored her cheeks. He started toward her. Her eyes widened, and she began fussing with her tunic, brushing off bits of clinging wool.

"You've never looked lovelier," he said as he offered her his hand.

She stared past his hand into his ice blue eyes and felt the very breath leave her body. His full, sensual lips curved into a wide smile. Her heart hammered in her ears while she reached up to accept his aid. When his hand closed around hers, the heat of his touch penetrated her fingers and spread throughout her body. She licked her dried lips as she struggled to think of something to say. The silence seemed to speak of its own accord, revealing the devotion growing for him within her heart.

"Have ye come for dinner?" she asked as he pulled her to her feet.

"Is that an invitation?"

His words sent her heart into a spiral. His rich, deep voice and the strange cadence of his speech surrounded her, filling her with a taste of distant shores and roads she would never travel.

"Would that please ye?" she said.

"At this moment, I care not for my own pleasure." He reached out and tucked a wayward lock of hair behind her ear. "My only concern is yours."

She could not contain her smile and decided then to leave off any coy affectations. "If it pleases my father, I would enjoy your company very much," she said as she instinctively drew a step closer. She had to suppress the sigh that came to her lips as she tilted her head back to meet his gaze, a rare pleasure, given she was nearly six feet in height.

A smile lit his face. Grabbing her fingers, he brought her hand to his lips. "Wait here," he said, intending to find Duncan and Brenna, but his search ended before it began. Her parents had already left their post by the fields and were standing just behind them. Clearly, they had watched Garik and Nellore interact with some interest.

Garik cleared his throat. He was a man of two and twenty. He had spent the past five years waging war against their enemies. He had stood beside Duncan in battle, and yet he did not think he had ever felt more nervous as he grappled for the courage to ask his fellow brother at arms for permission to join his family for dinner. Duncan would know his intentions. Hell, from the glint in Duncan's black eyes and the firm set to his jaw, he was already aware of Garik's intentions.

Garik bowed first, and then he stood to his full height and looked Duncan straight in the eye. "Duncan MacKinnon, could there be a place for me at your table this day?"

Duncan did not speak. He took a step closer, his eyes like steel daggers. Then a slow smile spread across his features while his hand came to rest on Garik's shoulder. "It would be an honor."

NELLORE TOOK A DEEP breath before she took up the bundle of hot oatcakes from the cooking table. Steeling her shoulders, she turned and strode over to the table where Duncan and Garik sat. She stared at the floor, the tabletop, the ceiling, anywhere but at Garik as she set the cakes down.

"Thank you," his said. His deep, lilting voice sent shivers up her spine. Her eyes darted to his face, and she smiled before she turned around once more, too breathless to reply.

"Breathe," Brenna whispered in her ear when she passed, carrying a steaming pot of rabbit stew.

"We've Nellore to thank for dinner," Brenna said as she placed the pot on the table.

"It smells delicious. Did you prepare it?" Garik asked, catching Nellore's gaze. She opened her mouth to speak, but the words remained lodged in her throat. She spun away, returning to the cooking table, trying to appear busy by dropping herring fillets in oat flour.

Duncan chimed in to save her. "'Twas Nellore who brought home the pair of rabbits, but do not let her skill with a sword fool ye, she is a wonderful cook."

Her nerves only worsened as dinner progressed. She longed to bury herself beneath her blanket while her parents carried on boasting with pride at her skills and attributes. She struggled over what to say, but it was Garik who lightened her mood. Duncan had made a jest about Garik's good humor and willingness to play the fool while they had been away.

"Whenever the atmosphere grew too melancholy among our men, Garik would get up to some trick or do something ridiculous."

"I'm not the only one who was willing to look ridiculous," Garik said, looking pointedly at Duncan. "I am speaking of the occasion we masqueraded as cattle."

"Cattle?" Nellore said, chuckling. "What on earth compelled ye to play at being cattle?"

Duncan threw his head back and laughed. "Lord James Douglas," Duncan said.

Garik's rich laughter filled her ears, warming her from the inside out. "Nellore," he said. "I swear what I'm about to tell you is true. At Lord Douglas's command, we wrapped our shoulders in black cloaks. With only the cover of night, we crawled on hands and knees toward the well-guarded curtain wall of a large castle. None of us were too pleased to leave behind the cover of trees and crawl like babies into the open. Dark or not, the garrison would've been able to see our movements, but James bade us not to worry. He assured us that the garrison would believe we were cattle. We nearly revolted, but he reminded us that under his command we'd successfully taken a dozen castles with only a small band of warriors. And in truth, the cattle scheme was not as outlandish as some of James's other plans, which had all been successful—"

Duncan cut Garik off then and continued with the tale. "We all thought we were done for, yet down we went on our knees, dragging our scaling spears behind us. We scattered throughout the grounds, pausing every now and then as James had bid. He said it would look as though we were grazing." Duncan turned to Brenna and brought her hand to his lips. "I had thought to myself—so this is the end of Duncan MacKinnon. Shot through by a crossbow, masquerading as a blasted cow."

"Did it work?" Nellore exclaimed and then she laughed. "Well, it must have worked, or else ye would not be sitting here with us."

"Indeed, it did," Duncan said with a wide grin. "Aye, your father can play at being a cow like no other."

"'Twas amazing, really," Garik said. "We were able to go straight up to the wall, and then upon James's command we jumped to our feet, raised our spears, and were scaling over the garrisoned curtain without anyone sounding the alarm. We were only thirty cattle strong—I mean men—and we took the castle."

Brenna snatched her hand from Duncan's. "I will hear no more of this," she snapped. "Ye will go off again and I will remain behind knowing your commander is a simpleton."

Duncan hooted with laughter as he moved to pour himself more ale, but Garik stayed his hand. From his satchel, he withdrew a jug.

"There is a tradition on the Orkney Islands," he said. "It is called the Speiring night." He cleared his throat. "In my language *Speir* means to ask."

Duncan stood up then and said, "Perhaps ye and I should take that jug outside and discuss some matters."

Garik nodded. Then he stood to follow but turned and winked at Nellore.

Rose gave Nellore a puzzled look. "Is a Speiring Night what I think it is?" she asked.

"Wheest, Rose," Brenna said gently. "Who's to know what a Speiring night is. I'd wager whatever it is, Nellore is at its center, but ye never know. The Orkney Islands are filled with all manner of queer traditions."

Nellore stared at the door. She could not remember ever feeling so nervous. Nearly an hour passed, and she feared the door would never open. But then Duncan peered inside. "Nellore," he said. "Will ye join us?"

Duncan took her hand and led her outside. "Ye will have to speak with Ronan on this matter, ye ken," Duncan said to Garik. "Ye can tell him that ye have my blessing." Then Duncan turned and dipped his head, pressing a kiss to Nellore's cheek. "Perhaps ye would care to walk Garik up the hill," he said. He grazed the back of his fingers gently across her cheek. "My dear, sweet lass. Ye're not a child anymore. Ye're a lion and a lamb all at once. I could not be prouder of ye."

Then he stepped back and stared into her eyes. Nellore felt as though he were saying goodbye, but not because of an expected absence. She could see in his eyes that he grieved for the passing of her childhood, the time when she was so essentially his—his own wee daughter. Admiration shone in his eyes. She felt as though he were seeing her as a woman grown for the first time. Tears wet her cheeks as she rushed into her da's arms. Childhood memories of his laughing black eyes and reliable strength flooded her mind, and she wondered whether she would ever know that same warmth again. Despite how well she loved Garik, she doubted the same security could be found in her true love's arms, for accompanying the comfort and security of a father is a child's innocence, which age all too swiftly snatches away.

"I love ye, Da," she whispered as she lifted her head from his chest. He smiled down at her. Then he cleared his throat and stepped away. With a sad shake of his head, he turned to go back inside, leaving her alone with Garik.

She eyed him shyly while she fidgeted with the belt of her tunic.

He stepped toward her, causing her heart to drum in her chest and her hands to shake. His eyes held an intensity that was palpable. He took another step forward, and the flurry of nerves that coursed through her forced her to speak. "What were ye and my father discussing?" she blurted.

A slow smile curved his sensual mouth. "Can you not guess?" he said as he drew ever closer. He reached out his hand and tucked her long black hair behind her ear. Then his fingers trailed down, grazing the sensitive skin of her newly exposed neck. She shivered and her breath caught in her throat.

"I only ken that which resides in my own heart," she said.

He drew closer still. Only a breath separated their bodies. Her head was spinning as she stared up into his eyes. Twilight colored the sky, and she decided that was his hour. The purple sky ushered in the moonlight, which set his black hair to glow with an ethereal light. His pale skin appeared even whiter, giving him the magical look of the fae. His ice blue eyes darkened with intensity. She licked her lips as her thoughts tumbled out of control. She was dizzy with the velocity of feeling and trembling and thinking that was setting her heart and mind to spin.

"Please," she said aloud, her voice pleading. Then she drew in a sharp breath as both of her hands rushed to cover her lips. She had not meant to speak and certainly not a word laced with such need. She was not even certain what she had sought with her beseeching outburst. She pursued his gaze, wishing to appeal to his judgment. Perhaps he could make sense of the storm brewing inside of her. But her lips parted when her eyes met his, releasing a sigh of wonder, for his eyes mirrored the tumult that writhed, cresting and falling, and soaring and diving within her.

Suddenly a low growl escaped his lips, and he wrapped his arms around her waist, pulling her close. She could not breathe or move. All she could hear was the pounding of her own heart. For years, she had dreamt of being enclosed within the warmth of Garik's embrace. The exquisite reality was almost more than she could bear. His smell surrounded her. His strength filled her. She slowly placed her hands on his chest and stared into the heat of his gaze. The world fell away. They stood cloaked in moonlight and shadow, swathed in the warmth of the summer night. And then his lips slowly descended to claim hers and she melted into him.

He crushed her against him. The feel of her soft mouth was more exquisite than he could ever have dreamed. She rose on her toes, eager to meet the demand of his kiss, and he surrendered to her will. He poured himself into her, wishing his kiss to hold the true promise of the devotion that filled his heart. Her lips burned through him, surrounding the hunger in his body and giving it greater life and feeling, until it consumed him with a need he had never known. His tongue caressed the curve of her bottom lip and she gasped, opening her mouth in invitation. His tongue stroked hers, and her hands went behind his head as she pressed closer. Her soft moans echoed inside of him, making him feel like he soared through the air with her in his arms.

He lifted her off the ground then and pushed her against the stone wall of her croft. Her legs came around his waist and her fingers laced through his hair. Dear God above, he ached with want. Fighting against his hunger to claim her, he tore his mouth from hers. She whimpered in protest as her lips once more sought his. He could not speak. His breaths came in great heaves. He turned then with her still in his arms and leaned his back against the stone. Shifting her in his arms, he cradled her and slid to the ground.

Some time passed while they sat together, she pulled close to his chest. Their breaths slowly quieted, along with their racing hearts. He pressed a kiss to her hair, and then he crooked his thumb under her chin, drawing her gaze to his.

"You are mine now, Nellore," he whispered.

She nodded her head as a smile spread her lips so wide it hurt. "Aye, Garik, I am yours," she said.

"Forever," he vowed.

She reached out her hand and cupped his cheek. "Forever," she promised.

Chapter Twelve

"Steady, Rose. Do not forget to breathe," Nellore said as she watched her sister pull her bowstring taught against her cheek. "Take aim with intent. Be deliberate. Fill your fingers with courage, and when you feel your mark, release the arrow."

Rose's sleek, strawberry hair hung in a thick braid down her back. Her small shoulder's strained against the strength of the bow, but Nellore watched her courage rise with her chest as she breathed the bowstring tighter and then released the arrow with her next breath. The shaft shot through the air and pierced the center of the target.

Rose squealed and threw her arms around Nellore's shoulders, her blue eyes wide with delight. Nellore swept her sister's petite frame into the air, spinning her around and around just as they used to do when they were lassies, as wild and free as the wind over the moors.

"What are we celebrating?"

Nellore recognized Logan's voice straightaway. She put her sister down and pointed to the target. "Rose has just been demonstrating her masterful skill with a bow."

She urged Rose to shoot again, but her sister discreetly refused while she fidgeted with the hem of her dress. Rose stared up at the sky and then out to sea. She seemed to look everywhere except at Logan. Nellore bit her lip to keep from chuckling as she recalled the night before when her own eyes had performed the same dance while she avoided looking at Garik.

"Ye needn't be shy," Nellore whispered. "'Tis just Logan."

Her words earned a scowl from Rose. "I see," Nellore said quietly. "So, my suspicions have been right. That is the way of it."

"Wheest," Rose whispered. "Please."

"Your secret is safe with me," Nellore said. Then movement behind Logan caught her eye. "Hello, Garik," she said, grabbing Rose beneath the arm. "Shall we walk the cliff line together?"

Garik offered his arm to Nellore. "It is a fine day for a walk," he said as he scanned the clear blue heavens and the gentle seas. She accepted his arm and gave Rose a gentle nudge toward Logan whose silver eyes lit up when Rose stepped his way. But then a sharp wind blew and swept his unbound silvery blonde hair across his face. He sputtered for a moment while he whipped his hair away from his eyes. Rose laughed at his struggle and reached up to help him.

"I should have tied my hair back on this windy day as ye've done," he said, reaching out and gently taking her long braid in hand. "Rose," he said in a whisper. Their eyes locked.

Nellore smiled at Garik. Then they quietly moved away together, leaving Logan and Rose to their staring.

"I've spoken to Ronan with your father's blessing," Garik said when they were alone.

Nellore's heart soared, but she contained her joy and gave him a quizzical look. "Oh, and what was the nature of your discussion?" she said. He threw his head back and the sound of his deep baritone laugh surrounded her. He grabbed her by the waist and pulled her close. "You," he said. "We discussed you and my lonely, empty hands."

She covered his hands with hers, which still gripped her waist. "Your hands appear quite full to me," she said. The words started off coy but then trailed off as she lost herself in the increasing intensity filling his blue eyes.

"Did our laird give ye his blessing," she asked softly as she rose onto her toes and brushed her lips against his.

"He did."

She wrapped her arms around his neck and seized him in a crushing embrace. She inhaled his scent. Happiness surged through her, but her bliss was short-lived. Just as her eyes opened and a new avowal of love rose to her lips, she spied something over his shoulder that stole the breath from her body. Tears rushed to her eyes. A ship sailed their way and at the helm she could see the crest of the Clan MacDonald.

"Angus Og has come for ye," she whispered.

Garik pulled Nellore tightly against him and then turned about to face the water. "So he has."

He looked down at her. "Do not surrender to fear. This changes naught. Our enemies have not the power to sway hearts. Nothing could ever alter my love for you—not absence...not even death."

"Ye must come back to me," she said, grabbing hold of his arms. "Swear it."

"I swear," he whispered. Then he pulled her against him once more and claimed her lips. His kiss raged through her, and she met the demand of his passion with a fury all her own. She could not imagine life without him. Pain squeezed her heart, her breath, and held her mind in a cage of terror as the insecurity of their future blinded her will. She squeezed her eyes shut and tried to compel the vessel and its banner of ill-tidings away.

Rose's gasp forced Nellore's eyes to open. She and Logan, who stood some feet apart, had spotted the ship. As tears welled in Rose's blue eyes, Logan reached out and placed a comforting hand on her arm.

Three days later, Nellore and Rose stood once more upon the cliffs of Mull, but this time without the men they held dear in their hearts. The ship nosed through the current, carrying their love into the mist. The future loomed dark and fierce, and from every angle she glimpsed suffering. She narrowed her eyes on the ship that, despite how her heart screamed, continued to diminish in size and fade into memory. A warning slunk between the vulnerable crevices of her mind. The world was on fire, and the flames would reach even the rolling moors of Mull.

Rain poured from the heavens, blending with the tears that coursed down her cheeks. Rivulets of muddy water captured tufts of bracken on their journey over the cliffs and down to the brisk waters below. She stared at the barren water, trying to conjure the image of the ship that had sailed out of view.

"I ken what ye feel inside," a soft voice said behind her. Nellore turned, meeting the courageous blue eyes of their mother. "Fear wells up from the pit of your soul. It steals your breath, and all ye wish to do is hide and forget the world until he is once more at your side."

Nellore turned away. Her sorrow swelled and writhed within her until she tasted bile churning in her stomach. "Do not ask me to move from this spot," she gritted. Fury rose up inside of her, competing against the sorrow for her soul.

"Ye cannot stand by and wait. No one's heart is strong enough to withstand the loss ye will feel with each breath that does not mingle with his, with every breeze that does not carry his scent, and with every wave that does not draw his ship closer."

Nellore shifted her gaze from the empty horizon to her mum.

"I know of what I speak. Your love is not the only one to have sailed away this day."

Nellore turned then and threw herself into her mother's knowing embrace. "How do I bear it," she sobbed. "How do I bear the unknown?"

"To love a warrior demands the strength of a warrior," Brenna said. "You will bear it because ye must."

Brenna's deep blue eyes met Nellore's with a willful, intractable spirit, but beneath the sensible calmness, Nellore glimpsed undercurrents of suffering. She took hold of her mother's hand. "My heart is not the only one to tremble with fear and need," she said while reaching to also take Rose's hand.

"Nay," her mother said quietly, her blue eyes now brimming with tears. Nellore's own heart quailed at Brenna's uncharacteristic display of sorrow. For the first time in her life, she saw Brenna not as mother but as a woman, a woman whose true love had once more been pulled from her side and sent hurtling toward danger.

"I've always longed to be a warrior so that I could fight for those I love most," Nellore said. "But I see now so clearly that which I have not understood until this moment. We *are* warriors, mum. Rose too, for we must fight to keep our minds and our homes at the ready for their return."

"Aye, dear heart," Brenna said as her hands swept tears from her eyes. "Come, ladies," she said. "Enough pining. The harvest is upon us."

Chapter Thirteen
The Mountains of Argyle, Scotland
Summer 1313

G arik stared up at the sky through the canopy of leaves overhead. The mountain air was cool and fragrant. He inhaled deeply and then closed his eyes, conjuring Nellore's image from memory. His eyes grazed over her long waves of black hair. The richness of her laughter soared through his mind, fueling his courage for battle.

"Seven years ago, our king and his fledgling army sought refuge in these mountains, but they found no respite," Angus Og said with his arms raised, directing the gazes of his men to the towering, jagged peaks that rose above the earth like grand sentinels. "Scots, Highlanders like ourselves, attacked our king. 'Twas the bastard MacDougall, the very chieftain who tried to steal MacDonald land."

Garik scanned the surrounding army of MacDonald and MacKinnon warriors. He stood out among the plaid clad men in his black leather jerkin, helmet, and mail, but then again, he was both Highlander and Viking; the ferocity of both peoples fed his blood.

"The fight for Scottish support of our King ends now, for the MacDougalls are the only remaining Scottish clan to give their fealty to the English king."

Nellore's image dissipated, drifting away on the breeze as Garik felt the immediacy of battle grip his body. His heart pounded, his hunger for justice stoked by his commander's every word.

"Ye've been given your orders," Angus Og cried. "Go now. Take to the mountains. Tear down these traitors to the Scottish crown."

Jagged boulders cut the mountainside. The narrow, steep passes and patches of dense wood would keep all English armies at bay, but they weren't looking for knights. They hunted for men not unlike themselves in appearance—Highlanders—but that was where all common ground ceased. Dishonorable conspirators to the English crown, the MacDougalls chose to make enemies of their own countrymen, but the end of their treachery was nigh.

Angus Og led the largest band of warriors straight up the mountain, their number sure to draw the enemy into battle. Under the command of James Douglas, Garik and a smaller band of only twenty men moved like shadows up the steepest side of the mountain. Running where the terrain allowed and scrambling over rock, they at last took position on the cliffs over the highest mountain pass where they hunkered down to wait.

Garik gained the ear of their leader. "Angus Og said the English have taken to calling you the Black Douglas," Garik whispered.

James grinned. "We've succeeded in scaring the English."

Logan appeared from behind and sidled next to James. "Lord Douglas, 'tis the MacDougall's," he said. "They are closing in on Angus Og."

"Ready yourselves, lads," James said.

Garik gripped his axe and waited. Every thought, breath, and beat of his heart trained on the forest below as he waited for the battle to begin. Then suddenly the forest came alive with terrific cries. They rose to their feet and with their own battle cries tearing from their lips they descended, pouring forth from tree limbs and rocks onto the MacDougall's below.

Garik charged with fury down the steep slope. Instead of skirting around a boulder jutting from the mountainside, he scampered on top of it and leapt through the air driving his ax into the neck of one MacDougall before flattening another to the ground. Blood splattered his face as his dagger carved through the man's neck, slicing it clean from his body. Jumping to his feet, he stayed low, ducking the swing of an enemy blade. Then he swung around and drove his dagger into the man's chest.

He released a mighty bellow before he reached behind his back and drew his sword. He fought as he was trained—without fear, without rules, and with a savage force that aroused his spirit. Another ruthless bellow tore from his lips as he leapt from rock to rock, carving his sword through limbs and bellies. He maimed and murdered like he was satiating a hunger, for he understood the demands of victory—instill fear, show no mercy.

Garik swung his blade, tearing across a man's side. The wound gaped open, releasing blood and organs. The man fell to his knees, still glowering up at Garik despite his fatal wound.

Garik growled as he shoved the man onto his back with his foot. Then he looked down at him and said, "I am Garik MacKinnon, and you are going to die. Your body will be feasted upon by the beasts of the forest." Then he raised his blade again in search of another wretch to slay, but the enemy was retreating, fleeing deeper into the woods.

"Nay," he shouted as he surged forward. He wanted to slay them all, but they were too far ahead. Raising his sword over his head, he hurled it into the trees. He cried out in victory as the blade wedged between enemy shoulder blades. His heart beat savagely as he turned his head to the sky and bellowed the MacKinnon battle cry to the heavens. Then Angus Og and his clan joined in with their own battle cry, and the air thundered with the sound of victory.

"'Tis done then," Angus Og said. "The last of Edward's Scottish supporters have been brought to heel.

They made camp at the foot of the mountain. The fervor of battle left Garik. He sagged into a clear spring, letting the water rush over his limbs, whisking away the blood and death that always left his heart cold. He closed his eyes and searched for Nellore's smiling green eyes amid the fresh images of war that choked his mind and his heart. He was a warrior, a fierce and fearless warrior, but he did not love the fight like so many others. His heart beat to a quieter rhythm and in that moment of peace and recovery he waited for the return of himself, the simple man who wanted nothing more in life than to love the woman of his heart. The release of his bloodlust ushered Nellore back into his soul. He closed his eyes and drew in a deep breath.

He longed for her. His heart ached in a way he never knew possible. In his mind, her scent still clung to his skin. She imbued his every breath and thought. As they marched onward, he thought not of the dangers ahead or whether he would survive. He thought only of Nellore. To him it was simple. She was his everything. His world began and ended within the tender warmth of her green eyes. He would continue to fight without fear because he did so to safeguard her life.

Chapter Fourteen
Isle of Mull, Scotland
Winter 1314

"Thank ye, Hamish," Nellore said.

"Whatever for, lass?" Hamish said as he turned to look at her with his one good eye.

"For letting me join ye today on your watch. 'Tis a fine day for a ride."

"Aye, brisk with winter's chill. Still, the sun shines. 'Tis a pleasure for an old codger like me to have a spirited lass at my side."

They rode over the moors, checking on cottars as they passed by. They even stopped to visit Mary and Gordon, who both had only good news to report. After waving goodbye, Nellore and Hamish set out once more, heading farther west to check the watch towers. As they approached the first tower, she pulled her horse to a halt and slid to the ground. She did not have to signal to Hamish. With an agility that belied his age, he dropped to his feet.

"Why is there only one," she asked as they eyed a lone MacLean warrior scaling the watch tower. "And where is the watch?"

"Mayhap, the watch saw the Maclean approach and has already ridden for aid," he said.

She squinted her eyes. She could see something in the tall grasses. "Nay," she cried. "The watch does not ride for aid." Fury coursed through her. She swung back onto her mount, ignoring Hamish's questions and protest. She kicked her heels into her horse's flanks and raced toward the tower, withdrawing her sword as she drew closer. The MacLean warrior atop the high tower had spotted her, but it was too late. He had nowhere to run. Swinging her sword with all her might, she sliced one of the tower's wooden legs. The sharp edge cut straight through. Then she circled back around and swung again, slicing through another leg. The tower, and the MacLean with it, came tumbling down.

Nellore leapt to the ground and raced past the MacLean who now writhed on the sodden earth, hugging an injured arm close to his body. Nellore paid him no heed. Her heart had been captured by the sight of her fallen clansman.

"Tavish," she called as she rushed to his side, but with a sharp intake of breath, she stopped short. "Nay, Tavish," she cried as she fell to her knees at his side. Three arrows protruded from his back. "God keep ye," she whispered.

"Where do ye think ye're going, ye murdering bastard?" Hamish growled. The MacLean had tried scurrying away on his stomach, but with only one good arm he had not made it far. Hamish flipped him over and drove his knee into his chest. Then he pressed his dirk against the enemy's neck. With satisfaction, Nellore noted the thin trickle of blood dripping down the MacLean's throat. She stared down into his wide, terrified eyes.

"I see ye trembling. Ye're wise to be afraid. Hamish would like nothing more than to dispense with your foul life right here, right now. I may be able to persuade him to bring ye to our laird, alive, if ye tell me where the rest of your band is," she said.

The MacLean swallowed. The action pressed his throat into Hamish's blade. "Keep breathing and ye just might skewer yourself," she said as the cut deepened, and more blood rushed down his throat. Nellore could see panic setting in.

"Look at me," she snapped. "Where are the rest of your men?"

"There...there...are none," he whispered.

'I don't believe ye," she said. "Press harder, Hamish. If ye want your head separated from your neck, then do carry on with your lies."

A frightened mewl escaped his lips as he whimpered, "I'm telling ye the truth. I...I'm a scout. The MacLean sent me to observe the watch, but your...your man saw me." The MacLean's eyes moved in the direction of Tavish's lifeless body.

"Tavish," she spat in his face. "His name was Tavish. Say his name," she growled.

Ta...Tavish. Tavish saw me. He was going to sound the alarm. I didn't know what to do—"

"So ye shot him in the back," Nellore spat.

"Ye know what that means, lass?" Hamish said.

She shook her head.

"The MacLean is planning a war. He monitors the watch to find any weak places by which to gauge the hour of attack."

Her eyes widened with surprise. Then she scowled down at the enemy. "Tie him up. We must take him to Ronan," she said.

They wrapped poor Tavish's body in his plaid and carefully slung him over her horse. She kept her arm over his lifeless body to ensure he did not slip. Meanwhile, Hamish tied their prisoner to the MacLean's horse, which he led behind as they road back to Gribun.

Gasps and outcries of rage announced their arrival in the village. Word spread quickly of Tavish's death. Soon, his heartbroken family surrounded Nellore. They lifted his body down and carried Tavish away, disappearing down a village path. They would bring him home one last time and prepare his body for burial.

Nellore wiped her tears and joined Hamish as he dragged their prisoner into the keep.

Ronan sat at the dais at the end of the great hall, listening to a dispute between two cottars. He held up his hand to silence the man speaking when Nellore and Hamish entered with their prisoner.

Nellore approached the dais, and without having to be told, the cottars bowed to Ronan and retreated from the hall.

"This man attacked the watch tower nearest the Cillchriosd Standing Stone. He filled poor Tavish's back full of arrows." A feeling of loss gripped her heart. For a brief moment, her laird's face mirrored her own grief, but soon sorrow gave way to fury. Ronan stormed over to the MacLean who Hamish had brought to his knees.

Ronan grabbed the smaller man by the hair and yanked him once again to his feet. "Just like a MacLean to stab a man in the back. Do ye deny it?" Ronan bellowed, his voice echoing off the high ceiling.

The MacLean shuddered, trying to pull away from Ronan's grasp as he cried, "Nay, I...I deny nothing."

"My laird," Hamish said, drawing Ronan's gaze. "He's a scout sent to monitor our watch."

Ronan brought the enemy's trembling face only a breath from his own. "Ye're planning a war," he gritted.

"Aye," the MacLean whispered, his eyes clenched shut against Ronan's fury.

Nellore followed close behind while Ronan dragged the broken man through the castle gates. "Go home, snake. Go home and tell your laird that we've learned of his plans and will be ready to fight." Then Ronan threw him down the wide, stone stairs. He landed before an angry mob that had gathered, hungry for justice. The enraged villagers wasted no time in grabbing hold of his arms. The MacLean flailed against the angry fists, calling out to Ronan. His words did not carry over the fury of the crowd, but Nellore gleaned enough to know the MacLean clung to information he believed of interest to the MacKinnon.

"Silence," Ronan roared. The tension in the air thickened when the villagers reined in their anger. Nellore held her breath as her chieftain turned back to the MacLean. "Speak," he said.

"My laird does not give these orders," he said. "The MacLean is ill. My orders came from his second son, Calum."

A widening of Ronan's eyes betrayed his interest, but he quickly recovered and stormed down the stairs. The MacLean quailed and hid his face in his hands. "I care not who is in command," Ronan roared. "Deliver my message. The message of the Clan MacKinnon. Tell the MacLean we are ready." Then Ronan held out his hands to his people, drawing their gazes. "Allow this man to pass," he shouted.

"But he is a murderer," someone yelled.

"Aye, but he carries my message," Ronan said, his eyes rising to challenge his people.

Without further protest, the villagers did as their laird bid and opened a path for the MacLean, but the enemy was not saved from a display of the peoples' wrath. A volley of refuse and spittle showered down upon the MacLean as he stumbled from the courtyard, cradling his broken arm against his chest.

"Forgive me, Ronan," Hamish said when they returned once more to the keep. "But we are in no position to fight a war."

Ronan's shoulders sagged. Suddenly, he seemed very old to Nellore. "I ken," he said quietly. After several moments passed and her chieftain still had yet to speak, Nellore grabbed hold of his hand. "What are we to do?" she said.

"Ye've done all ye can, Nellore. This hopefully will buy us some time. The MacLean will not attack knowing we wait for it. But if the bastard is intent on making war, then we've no choice but to send word to our men and pray the Bruce will be able to release at least some of our warriors."

Ronan stood then and wiped the fatigue from his eyes. "Hamish, ye send a messenger. Nellore, ye will walk with me, for I cannot be idle. I want nothing more than to bring that MacLean coward back so that I can send his head home in a box. A fitting end for a coward who would shoot a man in the back." He exhaled, offering his arm to Nellore.

"'Twould be folly, my laird, no matter how satisfying," she said. "We've not the arms to defend ourselves. Ye cannot give the MacLean a reason to bring the fight to our door."

He nodded and his amber eyes shone with admiration. "Ye truly are a remarkable lass. Ye're right, of course, though I wish it were otherwise."

She left the hall with her laird at her side. He led her through the gardens. She listened to him speak of earlier days while she considered the tenuousness of their position. A full attack would, indeed, be disastrous, but despite the ill-tidings of the day, within her grew a seed of hope that after two long years Garik might soon sail home.

Chapter Fifteen

It felt as though a lifetime had passed since Garik had last held Nellore in his arms. She had remained fixed in his mind. Even in the midst of battle when violent fury tore through him, she had been there—his light shining in the darkness. The taste of her had continued to linger on his lips, overpowering the iron taste of blood, which drowned the air when his knife cut through the muscle and sinew of his enemy. Countless eyes had closed forever beneath the might of his blade, but such is the price of freedom. They had not sought this war. It was not their greed that set the struggle in motion, but he, like the other Mull MacKinnons, would be damned before they'd relinquish their land and hearts without a fight.

And fight they had.

Their swords had gleamed with the blood of their enemy, but so too had tears been spent over fallen brothers. Continuous war had a way of reducing a man to shadow as he moved through a world starved of goodness, surrounded by death. The memory of Nellore alone had kept Garik whole in the face of so much suffering.

Under the leadership of Angus Og and Lord James Douglas, they had seized many of Scotland's strongholds, which had still been under English authority, and they did so with a fraction of the men and arms. The reasons for their success: the element of surprise and their ferocity. They attacked in the dead of night or under the guise of some elaborate ruse, and one stronghold at a time, England had been overthrown.

Still, despite their many victories, the fight was not over. King Edward's mighty army continued to march, and, most importantly, he still held Stirling Castle. Garik knew that more blood would be spilled over the fight for Scotland's independence, but at least for a short while he had a reprieve—not from war, for they journeyed home to face yet another enemy—but rather from the worst suffering of all: being separated from Nellore.

As soon as he had been able, Angus Og had granted Garik and the Mull MacKinnon leave to protect their village. It had been plain from Ronan's message that the MacLean tarried with more than just their stores. The MacKinnon warriors had been warned that they would have little time to secure Gribun; however, they had been released to do just that.

Garik dipped his oar into the water and thrust it forward and then back again with all his might. They glided over the still waters of the Sound of Mull, steering around patches of ice, but with Gribun so close, Garik did not feel the wintry chill. All he could feel was Nellore's sleek strength filling his arms. His whole body ached to hold her, to feel her, to tell her of the love he bore her. For a moment, a nightmarish thought crowded into his mind—did she still love him? Had she waited? Two years was, indeed, a long time to suffer someone's absence, but then he shook his head and reclaimed his oar, which he drove through the water. He would not doubt her love.

"Gribun," Logan shouted.

Garik stood from his seat and turned, spying the familiar port in the distance. The sun had just risen above the cliffs of Mull. Morning mist clung to the docks and rose from the shallows along Mull's shore. Dawn wove ribbons of color through fog and sea, which fanned out in glistening shades of gold and rosy hues.

"Row, ye eegits," Duncan shouted, a full smile straining the contours of his face.

The bell sounded. The watch had seen their approach. Soon the port would be teeming with villagers all eager to welcome them home.

Garik whirled around and picked up his oars. He rowed as if his very life depended on it, and in his heart, he truly believed it did. Nothing could wipe the smile from off his face. He hungered for her closeness. The thought of seeing her at long last filled him with the strength of ten men. He strained as he poured all his might into each row.

A roar of such joy erupted from the many onlookers as their ship drew into port. Cormac leapt first from the ship, landing straight into Anna's open arms.

Garik, Logan, and Duncan stood side by side, accepting the warm wishes and affectionate embraces from their kin, but the women they each longed for most were nowhere to be seen. Then Garik remembered the isolation of Duncan's home. It would have taken them longer to respond to the bell. Mist clung to the hill where she would first appear. He started to ignore the greetings of those around him, refusing to tear his eyes from the hilltop.

He heard her before he saw her.

"Garik," her voice called from beyond the mist. He surged forward, pushing through the throng of villagers.

"Nellore," he shouted, and then she emerged into the new dawn. Sun-kiss gold lit her flowing black locks, making them gleam with fire as she hastened down the hill. Patches of snow shone in the morning sun. Her hands gripped a plaid that hugged her shoulders, her only shield against the cold. As she raced, it spread out behind her like the wings of a graceful bird. Never had he seen anything so beautiful.

He barreled up the hill to meet her, and when she fell into his open arms a great sob shook her body and she cried out his name again and again. She melted into him, and he claimed her lips, kissing her with the flame of passion that had burned within him for so long. They clung to each other. He knew not where his body ended and hers began. Joyful laughter soon merged with tears of sorrow—an expression of the agony both had felt when the world had forced them apart.

He scooped her into his arms. She clung to him, burying her face in the crook of his neck. Still, he felt the tears stream down her cheeks. Garik passed Duncan who clung to his Brenna, both reveling in the joy of their reunion.

"Duncan," Garik said as he passed.

"Aye, Garik," he answered not tearing his eyes from Brenna's beautiful face.

"I am marrying your daughter," Garik called. Nellore threw her head back with laughter.

"As ye wish," Duncan shot back, adding his own laughter to their merriment.

Garik continued to carry Nellore across the moors toward her croft.

"Nay," she whispered as she cupped his cheek. "I do not wish to go home." Her fingers splayed out through his hair and then moved behind his head. She pulled his lips down to meet hers. Her tongue plunged into his mouth with bold, languid strokes. He groaned, filling her with fire. She deepened her kiss. She felt his strength surround her. For so long her life had been barren of true warmth, true joy. For two years, she had lain awake dreaming of his touch, his kiss, and his hands on her body. His smell ignited her with heat. She needed to feel him, to know that he was real, to know that he was hers. She wriggled from his arms and took hold of his hand, pulling him toward the wood.

"Where are we going? It is freezing out here. You will catch your death of cold."

She turned then and pulled him close. The yearning still trapped within her soul begged for release. "I do not plan on being cold for long," she said.

With a low growl he scooped her into his arms. "I shall keep you warm," he promised before passing through the trees.

He knew where he would take her, to a clearing beside a small brook. Snow lingered on the forest ground. The sun could not reach the white blanket to melt it away like it did on the open moors. The crunch of ice and the snapping of frozen branches announced their arrival as he picked his way through the woods. He set her on her feet and removed his cloak, which he laid on the ground, followed by his leather jerkin.

"This is how you were meant to be loved," she said. "Except the sun should be setting and not on the rise. For you are snow and twilight to me with your white skin and black hair and your eyes that gleam like blue ice."

He smiled, his white teeth shining like stars. "You are so beautiful," she whispered. He drew close and his hands gripped her sides. Slowly, his fingers trailed down her waist and over the curve of her hips, then back up the length of her torso to her breasts, which he gently cupped. His lips kissed hers and then traveled down her throat. "If I am twilight, then you are the moon in my sky," he whispered.

He swept the plaid from her shoulders and tossed it aside. They both reached for the others' clothing, their movements hurried and desperate. He ripped her belt from her waist and jerked her tunic over her head, letting the garments fall where they may. She grabbed his tunic and pulled it above his waist and up his chest. She stopped to kiss his skin, laving her tongue across the hard, taut ridges of his stomach. The surprise of her tongue against his skin shot through him, forcing a groan from his lips. His hands dug into her hair and he kissed her, bending her back. His mouth moved hard and hungry, his tongue stroking hers with passionate fervor. Her arms wrapped around his neck, and she pressed herself into his strength, her hands stroking across his thickly muscled shoulders. A deep moan escaped her lips. The years apart were forgotten. All she knew was him. He filled her. He was everywhere and in all things—in the air she struggled to breathe, in the new light and mist surrounding them. The pain and fear within her faded away and all that mattered was him.

His kiss broke away. His breaths were coming in great heaves as he stared down at her, but she did not meet his gaze. Her eyes raked over his naked body, boldly exploring every taut line and chiseled muscled. Then his lips upturned in a wicked grin while he reached for her. He groaned at the sight of her sleek strength as she stood before him clad only in her shift. Her breasts pushed taut against the thin fabric. He hungrily eyed the dark hue of her nipples. Her waist curved with graceful force. He could not contain his desire. His fingers came to the top of her shift and ripped it from her body. It fluttered to the ground like a secret whispered in the wood. The last barrier between her soft skin and his lay discarded in pieces on the ground.

He crushed her against him and groaned when he felt the fierce hold of her arms around his neck. He kissed her mouth and then down her throat, devouring a path of hunger across her breasts. Then he was on his knees, kissing her sleek stomach. His hands gripped her round, firm bottom while she raked her fingers through his hair. Soft groans drifted from her parted lips, fueling his passion. His lips and tongue trailed down her stomach and found the heat of her desire. He touched and tasted her until she writhed in his arms.

She trembled and shook. She did not think she could take anymore. His tongue stroked the very heat of her, making her cry out with need. A fire exploded within her, enflaming every inch of her body with wicked desire. The sweet, fiery ache grew until she thought she would burst with need. But then she felt his jerkin beneath her back, and he stretched over her. She opened herself to him and cried out when he filled her with his body. The years of longing guided their movements with desperate fervor as they pounded against each other. It was a struggle for oneness, a fight to unite in a way that would change them body and soul so that they might never be apart again.

Chapter Sixteen

S ilence resounded throughout the great hall when only moments before warriors had bellowed words of dissent while they debated how best to handle the threat of war from the MacLeans. Most wanted nothing more than to attack, ending the feud with a flurry of violence. However, Garik favored other solutions he viewed as more lasting. In the end, Ronan had silenced the debate with a stern reminder that while he still breathed air into his lungs, *he* was the laird of the MacKinnon.

"We shall lead a small party to meet with the MacLean," Ronan announced. Garik scanned the room. He exhaled when he realized none would dispute their laird.

"What sort of man is the MacLean?" Garik asked.

"He is a coward," Logan barked. "A greedy, feckless coward. We would be content to live in peace, but their chieftain is never satisfied. He hordes his stores and disciplines his clan too harshly, and so they work only to serve, which is just hard enough not to starve."

"Calm yourself, Logan," Ronan said. "Anger must not guide our actions. Now is the time for prudence. The only leader more unscrupulous than Darach MacLean was his father, Angus. But 'tis my belief Darach is not directly behind the latest attacks. He has not risen from his bed now for months, but while his health dwindles, his sons vie for power. I'd wager worse than that, he pits his sons against one another, challenging them to compete for the chiefdom rather than nurturing the rightful heir."

"Then the MacLean himself is an invalid?" Garik said.

"Aye," Ronan said. "The MacLean warrior who killed Tavish confirmed this."

"We should wait for their move and then attack," Logan said.

Ronan shook his head. "We've not the time to wait idly by. Remember, we await the call of our king."

Ronan's reminder made Garik's heart ache, but he swallowed the pain. Some truths hurt; still, they had to be faced.

"Our time here is limited. I would have us journey to Duart Castle and speak to the MacLean."

"What did ye mean by 'our' time?" Logan asked pointedly.

A rueful smile spread across Ronan's features. "I will be joining ye when the king calls once more, but for now I wish to propose a treaty with the MacLean that will establish a peace while we are away. He too swore his fealty to the Bruce. We march in the morning. Logan, gather the warriors, our number not to exceed ten. Most importantly, we do not wish our effort to be mistaken for a raid. We will carry our own colors but also the colors of the Bruce himself, for it is on his behalf that we make peace and remind the MacLean of the fealty he swore to Scotland."

DARKNESS STILL CLOAKED the courtyard as warriors assembled.

"Why have ye brought Nellore?" Ronan asked Logan.

"'Tis the very question I asked," Duncan snapped without looking at his laird. He was too busy glaring at Garik.

"Ye said 'twas essential our party not be mistaken for a common raid. With a woman in our company the peaceful purpose of our mission will be undeniable," Logan replied.

"The MacLeans are spineless blackguards who will think nothing of killing a woman," Duncan growled, shifting the sting of his gaze to Logan.

Garik stepped in between his friend and his soon-to-be wife's father, not liking the position at all. He cleared his throat. "Logan's idea has merit—" Duncan cut his words off as his hand came around his throat.

"If ye will so easily cast my daughter into mortal danger, then I have misjudged ye, Garik MacKinnon," Duncan snarled.

"Calm yourself, Duncan," Ronan said. "Logan's plan does have merit. Ye ken we are in no position to fight. If we march in a number great enough to make a strong defense, the MacLean will think we wage war. Should we appear as a raiding party, we will be outnumbered—lambs to the slaughter. With Nellore in our company and the king's banner flying overhead, the MacLean will have no choice but to grant us an audience."

Duncan continued to hold Garik's throat in a vice-like grip while he addressed his laird. "I will not allow my daughter to be the means to a questionable end."

"What would ye have me do?" Ronan said. "Invite war into our village, bring it to the doors of women not as capable as Nellore?"

Suddenly, the familiar sound of a sword being freed from its scabbard drew the men's gazes just in time to witness Nellore slice the air between Garik and Duncan, bringing the steel to a halt above Duncan's out-stretched arm. Despite Duncan's choking grip, Garik could not help but smile at the majestic wonder of his love. The wind swept her unbound, black curls into a dance about her hips.

"Da, let him go," she said.

Duncan's hand dropped straightaway, allowing Garik to breathe air into his lungs.

Nellore drew close to her father. "Ye ken I do not do this to be defiant, nor am I blind to the risks. But, da, our lives are marked by war. Perhaps one day peace will come but not without sacrifice. Peace is a hard-won struggle as ye well know. Ye *will* be called away once more to fight. Now is the time to safeguard Gribun."

"She comes," Ronan said. His tone held a finality even Duncan could not ignore. Then an amber glow lit Ronan's brown eyes as he smiled. "Besides," he said, "Nellore could best any MacLean warrior. Hell, 'tis likely she could best any of ye."

Duncan nodded but worry clung to his features. Garik drew close and put his hand on Duncan's shoulder. "I told Logan he was a fool when he first spoke of bringing Nellore. I threatened to beat the idea from his head. But then he reminded me of the woman I love. She's no average maid. You know it as well as I." He started to walk away, but then he called back to Duncan. "I will let nothing happen to her. This I vow."

NELLORE BREATHED IN the crisp, wintry air as they set out from Gribun. She cast her da a sideways glance. His brow was set to brood, but she could not blame him after the tongue-lashing Brenna had given him when she learned Nellore was to be included in the band of warriors traveling south to their enemy's territory. Nellore had tried to calm her mother's ire, but to no avail. It was their lady, Bridget, who had been able to convince Brenna of the wisdom of their plan. Nellore had overheard the words Bridget used to comfort Brenna—they were words that now echoed in Nellore's mind and sent shivers down her spine.

"Remember, Brenna, we each have a destiny. Do not stand in Nellore's way. The stars revealed her place in our clan long ago. The destiny of our clan is tied to her. Let her go," Bridget had said.

With talk of the stars and destiny and the fate of their people in her hands Nellore had set out with her lover on one side and her father on the other. She had never been farther south than Benmore Mountain. The closer the mountain loomed, the faster her heart pounded. Although she was afraid, she held tightly to the conviction that pulsed through her—the knowledge that everyone had a duty to the clan, and more than anything she longed for the peace that would keep Garik alive and at her side.

Snow began to fall. She and Garik pulled the hoods of their cloaks over their heads, while the other warriors enclosed themselves within their plaids. After several hours spent crossing moors and winding though narrow forest roads, they descended from a hill that had given them a distant view of Duart Castle. Surrounded by water on three sides, the narrow yet tall stronghold was better fortified than Nellore would have guessed.

Another forest spread out before them. Clumps of snow fell from the thick canopy of fir branches, which lined the narrow road. She slanted her eyes to glimpse the fineness of Garik's profile. He had removed his hood. She longed to wind her fingers deep into the thickness of his long, black hair and pull his face down to meet hers. As if sensing her gaze, he suddenly turned to look at her. A slow, deliberate smile told her he had guessed the sensual nature of her thoughts.

"The snowflakes clinging to your hair give you the appearance of an angel," he said. Then he lowered his voice to a whisper, "Though I know you are no angel."

She smiled and warmth flooded her cheeks as she blushed, but her avowal of love was stolen from her lips by an arrow that whizzed past her head. Her breath caught, and her mind emptied as instinct took over. She kicked her heels into her horse's flanks and joined the other warriors as they raced forward. Behind them the sound of the MacLean battle cry rent the air.

Just ahead, she spied another warrior through the trees with his bow drawn. She did not hesitate. Before drawing her next breath, she gripped her horse's sides tightly between her thighs and pulled her bow string taut against her cheek. Releasing her arrow, she watched it find its mark. The warrior fell from the banking onto the open road. They charged forward. The fallen MacLean's bones snapped beneath the pounding of her horse's hooves. Then the trees came alive. MacLeans descended upon them. She was knocked to the ground by a heavy man who had dove at her from a high place in the trees. She landed with a hard thud. The wind left her lungs. She struggled to breathe and fought to move the bulk of the stout warrior sprawled atop her. At last, she wriggled free, but before she had time to right herself and draw her sword, the MacLean had the point of his dirk pressed against her throat.

"I have the lass," he shouted above the clashing of steel. "I will kill her. Put down your arms or watch while I slit her lovely white throat."

Her eyes darted from left to right, scanning the battle. Her kinsmen dominated the fight, but when the MacLean's words reached their ears, they ceased their struggle.

"That's right," the MacLean snorted. She looked up at her captor. He was short and stout of build with a bulbous nose and breath that reeked of onions.

"Get your hands off of her," Garik shouted. Three MacLean blades pressed against his chest, but still he growled his protest. "I will rip out your heart," he snarled.

The distasteful little man leered down at her. "Stand up, whore. I would see all of ye before I slit your throat." She stared up at him, her face impassive. She moved to her knees and then slowly stood to her full height. His eyes were as wide as saucers as they traveled from her toes to the top of her head. She towered over him.

"Surprised?" she said softly the instant before she thrust her knee into his groin. He crumpled to the ground. All at once, the MacKinnon warriors raised their swords. A MacLean charged at her, but she reached behind her back and withdrew her blade. Whirling around, she sliced her attacker across the belly. Then she turned and drove her steel into the chest of another. He stumbled back and then fell to ground, dead. She stormed to his side and pressed her foot into his bloody chest, withdrawing her blade in time to parry the blow of yet another MacLean coming at her from the side.

"Back to back," Garik shouted to her. She nodded charging forward. When she reached his side, she turned so her back was to his. The din of steel on steel echoed around them. Within a matter of minutes, the MacKinnons had the MacLeans bested.

"Did ye see the look on that eegits's face when ye stood to your full height?" Logan said between bouts of laughter. "I thought he was going to faint dead away."

"In the end, I think he wished he had," Hamish said.

"Aye, my fierce lass," Duncan said, smiling as he pulled Nellore into his arms.

"She took them all by surprise," Ronan said.

Garik's hand smoothed down her hair. She turned to face him. "Are you all right," he whispered as he tucked a stray black lock behind her ear. His hands skimmed over her body, looking for any injury.

"I am fine," she said. "I assure ye."

"I am just making certain. I've seen it many times, men with holes in their bellies, but they are too numb to know they are injured." Garik was the only man, including her father, not celebrating their victory. She reached out and cupped his face in her hands, forcing her eyes to meet his. "I am well, not a scratch. I swear it," she said.

He stared at her for several moments. Fear surrounded him in an anxious shroud. Then he clutched her close, squeezing her so tightly she could hardly breathe.

She stroked a soothing hand down his back and pulled his head down so that her lips grazed his ear. "Ye've naught to fear, my love," she whispered. Then she pressed her lips to his. He returned her kiss with an ardor that sent a shock of sensation coursing throughout her body. She tasted the power of his fear. She knew then that he had seen the MacLean dirk against her throat and thought the worst. She tore away from the power of his kiss.

"I'm alive." Her hand rested on his chest. She could feel his heart still pounding.

"Garik," she said. "Look at me. I am alive." His blue eyes met hers, and she melted against him. "I love ye," she whispered.

"Garik," Ronan said behind them. "Pull yourself together, man. The lass is fine."

Garik tore his eyes from hers and nodded to Ronan. Then he looked back at her. "You do not leave my side until we are back at Gribun. Do you understand?" he said. He did not wait for her reply. He swung her into his arms and put her on his horse. Then he pulled himself behind her. She leaned her back into his chest and savored his heat. His arms gripped her possessively as they rode toward Duart Castle.

Chapter Seventeen

"If ye wish to enter the keep, ye will leave your weapons," a MacLean's guardsmen said.

"I heard ye the first time," Ronan answered, although his hands remained crossed over his chest.

"Ye've ten men with ye," the Guardsman replied. "'Tis a great enough number to take a few of us with ye to Hell before we slaughter the lot of ye."

"Nine men," Ronan said. Then he jerked his head toward Nellore. "We have a woman in our company."

The guardsman seemed to notice her for the first time. "So ye do," he said thoughtfully. Then he retreated a few steps to where another guard stood at attention. After they exchanged a few inaudible words, the second guardsman disappeared through the gate.

The guard remaining continued to stare Ronan in the eye but said nothing.

Within a few minutes, the second guard returned. "Come on then, ye've been permitted inside, but ye ken ye're surrounded."

They stepped into the keep.

At the high dais sat two men. One was not altogether unpleasant to look upon with his broad shoulders and blonde hair paired with thick, black brows. His sharp, dark eyes seemed to follow every movement in the room. The man next to him had the same coloring but a sickly countenance. He did not bother to look up from his meal as they entered.

"State your business," the larger man said.

"We are here to see the MacLean," Ronan replied.

The man's sharp eyes flitted over Ronan and the rest of the MacKinnons before he rose. Only then did the smaller man at his side look up. His thin face bore a vacant expression. She could tell they were brothers, but more than that, judging by the frail man's indifference to the MacKinnon presence in the keep, she knew he was the younger and less valued son. Her eyes shifted back to the taller man. A sneer curved his lips. He came and stood before Ronan.

"The MacLean will not see ye," he said.

"Ye mean he cannot see me," Ronan replied. "I ken he's taken to his bed."

The man shrugged, clearly unconcerned for his father's well-being.

"Ye must be Balfour," Ronan said.

Balfour only nodded in reply.

"The warrior ye sent to my lands, the one that filled my kinsman's back with arrows, was good enough to inform me of your father's condition."

The MacLean paused. She saw his lips twitch, hinting at a smile, but it left as quickly as it came. "Ah, yes, I had forgotten about that matter," he said.

"I assure ye, I have not," Ronan snapped.

"Save your ire, MacKinnon. That man did not act on my command or my father's. My brother, Calum, has ambitions which can be trying to contain."

"Perhaps there is something I can do to help ye contain, as ye put it, your brother's ambition. We've come here in peace. The presence of a lady in our number attests to this."

The slamming of a door echoed throughout the hall, causing her to jump with surprise. "He lies," a voice shouted from behind the screen, which she assumed separated the high dais from the family rooms deeper in the keep. She strained to see who spoke, but then the foul man who had threatened her life in the forest strode into view. When he saw her, his face twisted with anger. "And that is no lady. She just struck down three of our men. Look at the size of her. She wields a blade with the strength and skill of a trained warrior."

Garik pushed her behind him as he turned to face the accuser. She peered around his shoulder and studied the man shouting his way through the great hall. His deep baritone voice echoed off the high ceiling.

Ronan shifted his gaze away from the naysayer. "As I am sure you well know, Balfour, we were set upon in the woods. Given no chance to declare our position, we were forced to defend our lives. I do not deny this lass has some skill with a blade. It is by my decree that all MacKinnon women know the finer points of weaponry. I do not believe in allowing women to be defenseless."

"Again, he lies," the man said as he joined Balfour. "They attacked us."

"Yet, ye somehow managed regrettably to escape, Calum," Balfour said dryly.

Calum ignored Balfour's disdain. "Only just."

"A pity," Balfour said before turning back to Ronan. "I would thank ye for sparing my brother's life, but ye did me no real favor. Still, I will hear ye out, Ronan, laird of the MacKinnon."

"I seek a treaty with your clan, a sort of temporary peace," Ronan said.

"And why would we grant ye this, now, when our power is growing and victory is nigh."

"Ye're mistaken if ye think ye have the might to take my lands," Ronan said. "If my will was guided by greed, I could take from ye all that ye see," he said, lifting his arms to encompass the whole of the great hall. "But I care not for your lands. I wish only to nurture my own people. The only reason your tinkering has gone unanswered is because my warriors have been occupied visiting hell upon another foe, a common enemy to both the MacLean and MacKinnon clans," he said.

Then Ronan grabbed the banner of the king from Hamish's hand and thrust it toward Balfour. "Our king," Ronan began, "the very king ye swore fealty to at Scone, has called his loyal subjects to war. Now is the time to take back our lands from the English. This is not a struggle for Mull. This is a fight for Scotland."

"What do you seek from me, old man?" Balfour said.

"A promise of peace."

Her eyes followed Calum who had stood and whispered something in Balfour's ear, but Balfour shoved him aside with a look of fury on his face. "My brother advises me to end this feud now and slay every one of ye."

The sound of steel being released echoed through the great hall as every MacKinnon held their sword or ax at the ready. "Put down your weapons," Balfour said. "Thankfully, my feckless brother does not command my clan. I will grant ye your peace."

"What about the recent attacks?" Ronan asked.

Balfour jerked his head at Calum. "He is a drunk, nothing more. There was no real will behind his efforts." Calum's eyes bulged with anger, but he made no attempt to stand up to his brother. He simply turned on his heel and stormed past the dais and disappeared once more behind the screen.

A smirk played at Balfour's lips as his eyes followed his brother from the room. Then he turned back to face Ronan. "When the time comes, I too will march with my men for the Bruce. Ye can rest assured that both of my brothers will be joining me. That idiot there making love to his meal is my youngest brother, Finnean."

Nellore glanced over at the high table. The small man did not look up as he shoveled another spoonful down his gullet.

"Not that Finn is much of a threat to anything more than a plateful of bannock," Balfour said, laughing, but then his expression grew serious as he stepped closer to Ronan. "I will not lie to ye," Balfour said. "I want your land. One day it will be mine. Ye can expect a different sort of attack from me when I'm laird, but I can hardly take control over Mull with the English breathing down my neck." He raised his cup. "Drink with me, Ronan. Drink to secure our treaty. While we are away fighting the English, the Maclean will leave the north of Mull in peace." He took a sip and then passed the cup to Ronan. "For Scotland," Balfour said.

Nellore breathed the tension from her shoulders while she watched her laird share a cup with their enemy. Despite Bal-

four's threats, a belief in the possibility of peace laid claim to
her heart.

Chapter Eighteen

Nellore shivered. The new moon cast the courtyard of Dun Ara Castle into shadow. Garik's hand pressed against the small of her back, urging her up the wide, stone stairwell and into the keep. Three days had passed since their excursion into enemy territory, three blissful days spent shirking as much work as possible while she savored her time with him; however, that night, when darkness had descended on Mull, an ill wind cut through her clothing with its icy fingers. She had tried to dismiss the notions of foreboding, but then a messenger had arrived from the keep, summoning her family.

"We leave by week's end," Ronan announced, his voice booming throughout the great hall.

Nellore stumbled back. His words had pained her no less than a physical blow. Just when Garik had been returned to her, she was to lose him again. She had known his time on Mull would be short, yet Ronan's words tore through just the same. Perhaps, she had tricked her mind and heart into believing he would remain forever at her side. Her mind glimpsed the nights and days ahead—weeks, months, dear God, even years of suffering his absence, not knowing whether he lived or died.

The room began to spin. Fear clutched her heart. She fought to maintain control as she scanned the hall. She found her mother. Brenna's features betrayed a whisper of pain that broke through her famed composure, but knowing her mother as she did, Nellore knew the true depths of the heartache Brenna fought to conceal. Then Nellore spied Rose, who stood alone with her sadness while she stared with longing across the room at Logan. The object of her unspoken affection was busy speaking with Ronan, but as if he sensed Rose's gaze, he turned abruptly. Nellore watched as Rose and Logan stared at each other, their gazes filled with regret and yearning.

Nellore closed her eyes and prayed for strength. She knew she did not suffer alone, and she was determined to be strong—strong for her mother, for her sister, for so many of her kinswomen who, like her, were fated to watch their men fade into the mist, hoping above all hope that they would return.

"Breathe," she said aloud. The spinning in her mind slowed, allowing her to master the pounding of her heart. She closed her eyes and took a deep breath. Then she lifted her lids and met Garik's wintry gaze. A quiet smile warmed their ice blue depths. "Do not mourn my absence yet," he said softly as he brushed away a single tear that trailed down her cheek. "For we've much to do."

"Aye," she nodded while she swallowed down the remainder of her tears. "We must ensure ye've bannock and dried meat for your journey."

He smiled down at her. "At this moment in time, I am not at all concerned about the journey. How could I be when we've a wedding to plan?"

"What wedding?" she said, and then her eyes grew wide. She threw her arms around his neck, and he lifted her off the ground.

"I mean to marry you before I leave," he said softly. His lips grazed her ear as he spoke, sending shivers up her spine.

She drew back a little to look into his eyes. The love he bore her poured forth from his gaze, filling her with well-being. She entwined her fingers through his hair and pulled his lips hard against hers. The urgency with which she kissed him set her heart racing once more. She felt as though she were gasping for life as she hungrily sought his lips for more. She could not bear to lose his touch again. Tears sprang to her eyes. She tore her lips from his. He let her feet touch the ground, and then he clutched her close.

"Hush, my love," he whispered. "It is the eve before our wedding. I would have you happy."

His eyes held all the heartbreak she felt, but they also shone with hope. "Be my wife," he whispered.

"Aye," she blurted as she smiled through her tears. "There is nothing I want more," she said. And then her tears were overtaken by laughter.

He smiled down at her. "Why do you laugh?"

"There is yet one thing ye must do," she said.

He cupped her cheeks and slowly kissed her lips before vowing, "Anything, my love, all you need do is ask."

"Nay, Garik, 'tis ye who need to do the asking," she said. "We need my father's permission."

He drew back slightly. "Yes, you are indeed right. I admit I had not considered that. Well, we've had the Speiring Night," he said, causing her to laugh even harder when she remembered the night Garik had paid her father a visit with a jug of ale to ask for her hand in marriage. "True," she said. "But ye do not have his consent to marry me so soon."

"So soon?" he said. "We've been betrothed for two years."

"Aye," she said, "most of which we've spent apart."

"I see your point," he said. Then he winked at her and grabbed her hand. He led her through the crowd of anxious villagers toward her parents who were standing quietly in the rear of the great hall. Duncan wore a sad smile on his face while he held Brenna and Rose in a strong embrace.

"Duncan, I have a boon to ask of you," Garik said, pulling Nellore close to his side. "I wish to marry your daughter."

"I believe that is one boon I've already granted ye," Duncan replied.

"Yes, you have," he agreed, his eyes flitting from Duncan to Nellore and then back to Duncan. "But, you see, I wish to marry her tomorrow."

Duncan's eyes widened with surprise but then narrowed. "There's no time. We've naught prepared. God's blood, man, ye haven't posted the banns."

Brenna cleared her throat. "Duncan," she began, "if ye recall, we did not exactly have time to post the banns of marriage before we wed."

"Aye, Da," Nellore chimed in. "Ye told me the story yourself of your unplanned nuptials."

Duncan arched a brow at Nellore. "In our particular case, I was near death when we exchanged our vows. In truth, I do not remember the entirety of my wedding." Then with a sigh he said, "But I will concede there was certainly no time to post the banns."

"Have ye any other objection?" Garik asked.

Brenna and Duncan exchanged glances. Then they both smiled. "Ye have our blessing," Duncan said.

Garik threw his head back and whooped. He cupped his hands around his mouth and shouted above the din of the great hall. "There is going to be a wedding. I marry Nellore on the morrow."

The hall erupted with cheers. In moments, Bridget and Anna were at her side and wedding plans ensued. Rose squeezed Nellore in an enthusiastic embrace. "Ye will be the most beautiful bride," she said, promising to put the finishing touches on Nellore's wedding clothes. Anna put herself in charge of decorating the kirk and Ledaig House. "I love winter weddings," she said, her silver eyes dancing. Then she leaned in and placed a kiss on Nellore's cheek before darting from the hall. Soon Nellore was swept away on a wave of her womenfolk with Brenna and Bridget in the lead.

That night Nellore soaked in a bath scented with lavender oil. She felt surrounded by the blessing and magic of her clan. All the ladies had set to baking and cooking for the morrow's feast. Despite the scarcity of time, Bridget swore there would be joints of beef, rabbit stew, barley, and plenty of bannock. The sun was not far from rising when Nellore, Brenna, and Rose at last settled down to sleep in a room in the keep.

Nellore's eyes sprung open when a sliver of light crept through the closed casement, announcing the sun's arrival. She leapt to her feet and rushed to wake her mother and sister.

"Morning could not have come soon enough," Rose said, laughing as she hastened to gather up the bride's wedding clothes. Nellore stood while Brenna, Rose, and Bridget dressed her. She wore a soft green tunic embroidered with yellow flowers at the neck, a belt with golden threads, and a cloak of emerald, the hood of which was adorned with fur.

Brenna smiled, her deep blue eyes alight with tears. "Ye're a vision," she said as she stood on her tip toes and rested a garland of holly on Nellore's unbound, black curls.

All eyes shifted toward the door when they heard a soft rapping. "'Tis time, ladies," Duncan said, peering inside.

On her father's arm, Nellore waited while the doors of the great hall opened. The sky was bright, despite the veil of white clouds obscuring the mid-morning sunshine, and a soft snowfall dusted the village and the surrounding moorland. They left the keep, walking down the wide, stone stairwell and then through the castle gate beyond the courtyard. Her clan already lined the village path leading to the kirk, and when she appeared, they began to cheer. They had no flower petals to throw. Instead, they waved pine branches, the emblem of their clan, as she passed. After, they fell in line behind her. As the procession grew, so too did her excitement until she felt she would nigh burst with joy.

When they neared the kirk, she spotted Mary who jumped with glee. Nellore waved and called out in greeting to her dear friend. And then a flash of red darted toward her. Maggie, now five years old, threw herself into Nellore's arms. Nellore laughed and kissed her before Mary pulled the wee lass back into line.

Nellore turned then and faced the kirk. There he was. Her heart swelled at her first sight of Garik. He wore his finest black leather jerkin, a belt embroidered with silver threads and a black cloak hung about his broad shoulders. The smile on his face made her knees weak. It was all she could do to keep from throwing herself into his arms just as Maggie had done to her only moments before.

Duncan must have sensed her sudden desire to race forward because he smiled down at her. "Steady now. We are almost there, lass."

Laughter burst from her lips. "Ye ken me so well, Da," she said before pressing a kiss to his cheek. She could not remember a time when she felt more full of life or more aware of the true blessings of a heart well-loved.

At last, the stone steps of the kirk lay behind her and she stood face to face with the man she had loved since she was naught but a child. She stepped away from Duncan and threw her arms around Garik. Joyous laughter spread throughout the gathering as he swept her into his arms and kissed her long and hard.

The priest cleared his throat. "We've not come to that part yet," he said with a glint of mischief in his eye. He did not begrudge the young lovers their happiness.

Nellore gave the Mass its solemn due, and when the priest prayed for the Lord to bless their union, she whispered her own prayer for Garik's safe return. Her hand trembled while she extended her finger to receive his promise. As he slid a band of silver in place, the priest's words filled her heart. "Remember, Garik and Nellore, that a ring has no beginning and no end just as your love must have no beginning and no end."

Nellore's heart soared. At long last, they were wed. "Now is the time I know ye both have been waiting for," Father Conall said before turning toward the groom. "Garik," he said. "Ye may kiss your bride."

He pulled her into his arms and kissed her with a passion that seethed from deep within his soul. Everything disappeared except for her, every cheer from the pews, the tolling of the bell.

It all faded and for that moment there was no war, no threat from the MacLeans. The only thing that existed was their love. But the moment ended too swiftly. The doors leading out of the kirk swung open and the merriment began. It pained him to lift his lips from hers, but their kinfolk were ready to celebrate.

They made their way to the Ledaig House. Holly and evergreens hung from the beams. In the hearth a fire roared and upon the table steaming trenchers of food awaited the revelers. Garik escorted Nellore to the head table, and then with a kiss he promised to return. From within one of the storerooms at the rear of the hall, he found what he had hidden early that morning.

"Attention," he shouted while making his way back into the hall. Above his head he raised an over-sized wooden cup with several long handles extending from around its rim. "My friends," he said. "This is a cog. On the Orkney Islands a wedding is not a wedding unless a cog is continuously being passed about, from which all must drink. We do this to ensure everyone partakes in the joy of our union. To you, my love," he said to Nellore before he gave her the cog from which to sip.

Logan, who was seated at Garik's side, accepted the cog from Nellore. He raised it high before he drank. "Speaking of wedding traditions. I believe I ken why ye made to marry so soon," Logan said before passing the cog onto Duncan.

Garik raised his brow at Logan. "Is there another reason besides the infinite love in my heart and our imminent departure?"

"Aye, ye wished to escape the creeling," Logan said.

Garik laughed. "Do you mean that cruel torture where the groom is forced to carry a backbreaking load of rocks around the village until he's nigh ready to collapse?"

"Aye, that 'tis the one," Logan said, smiling. "I might see fit to force the creeling upon our return."

"Agreed," Garik said. "Either way, I get off easy. On the Orkney Islands we have a far more dastardly tradition."

Logan raised a skeptical brow. "What could be worse than the creeling?"

"I will let you be the judge," Garik said. "To begin with, they strip the man of all clothing, regardless of the season and then bind him with rope and douse him in honey."

"Sweet Jesus," Logan gasped.

"It does not end there," he said. "Then they roll the poor sap's naked, sticky body in a pile of grasses and feathers. And if that is not enough, he is paraded through the village on a wagon while all the unmarried louts who tortured him to begin with beat drums and shout and draw as much attention to his feathered arse as they can."

"Are you lying to me?" Logan asked.

Garik shook his head while he tore off a piece of bannock and dipped it in the thick stew. "It is called the blackening, and it is one tradition I am damned grateful to be spared."

"I think I'd become a priest rather than face that ordeal," Logan said.

Garik picked up his tankard and raised it high. "To marrying a lass from Mull."

After several merry hours of feasting and dance, Garik leaned close and whispered in Nellore's ear, "The celebration will carry on until the morrow whether we linger or not."

Her eyes filled with a hungry glint, but he knew her appetite for food had already been sated. "I've never been inside your house," she said before pressing a long kiss to his lips.

He stood and extended his hand for her to accept. "Let us go home."

Chapter Nineteen

With Garik at her side, Nellore hastened through the village to escape the chill of the night. Relief from the cold was hers the moment she stepped into his home. A warm fire crackled, imbuing the air with currents of heat. She wandered around the large room, stopping to run her fingers across a beautiful table, and then it dawned on her—this was now her home, her table. She smiled as her fingers curved over the intricately carved detail.

"Did you make this?" she said, looking up. She found him studying her from across the room.

He nodded in reply.

"'Tis beautiful," she said as she once more stroked the fine wood. Peering through her lashes, she saw a pleased smile tug at his lips. His workmanship was extraordinary. While she studied the complexity of the carvings, her heart grew heavy.

"What is it," he said. "You seem sad."

She flashed him a smile. "On the contrary, I've never been so happy. 'Tis just that I did not know ye could do this," she said, gesturing to the finely made furnishings. "I suppose there must be many things I still have yet to learn." She fought against the despair that pushed to the fore of her thoughts. He would be gone from her side sooner than later, taking the secrets of his life with him.

"Come here," he said softly, holding out his hand for her to accept. He pulled her toward the far end of the room, which he used as a workshop, and then he placed a wooden plane in her hand.

"Have you ever shaped wood?" he asked. She shook her head. She had never even held a plane before. It was long and not overly thick and surprisingly heavy for a wooden tool, but then she peered inside and spotted a sharp metal edge.

"Here," he said, placing a short wooden stool before a thick cut of wood, "have a seat." The bark had already been stripped away and the top was leveled but still rough. "Place the plane blade side down." She laid the plane on the wood. He knelt behind her on one knee. His arms came around her, and he showed her the proper way to grip the tool. "Now smooth the wood," he said. She pushed the plane across the surface, peeling away a thin layer of fiber. The smell of freshly cut wood teased her nose, and she inhaled the scent.

"Push down harder," he said. "It takes a strong back to carve and shape wood."

His hands covered hers, and together they pressed the metal edge deep into the log. Blonde, wooden curls fell to the ground and began to collect at their feet. She found the action very pleasing. "'Tis wonderful," she said.

"Indeed, you are," he whispered in her ear.

She laughed and swatted him playfully. "Ye ken I meant the wood," she said.

He kissed her then and pulled her to her feet. "I've often thought of you when I've sat here working late into the night with only the fire to guide my hand. Time and again, I wondered whether you would enjoy working the wood. There are greater purposes for a pair of strong hands than gripping a sword, Nellore."

"Ye'll have to show me more," she said. "What are ye making?"

"A new chest for your garments and linens."

Her eyes widened with delight. "Thank ye, Garik, but ye ken ye don't need to fuss over me?"

"I know," he said, "but I like to."

"Well, then, I won't complain," she said as she began to survey the rest of her new home.

"What are these?" she asked, picking up one of several small, wooden figures from the table. He drew close.

"They are Viking gods. That is Odin. He is the god of war and of wisdom and magic."

She smiled, returning Odin to the table. "And who is this," she said.

"That is Freyr. He is the son of the sea god. He is the god of virility and prosperity. This is his twin sister, Freyja," Garik said, showing her a different figure.

She returned the wood carvings to the table, and then her hands gripped the belt at his waist. "I must remember I've married a Viking," she said as she pulled him close and pressed herself against his hard chest.

"Aye, ye have," he said, imitating her accent. "And I've married a fine Scottish lass." He stroked his finger down her cheek and whispered, "Jeg elsker deg," threading his fingers through her hair.

"What did ye say?" she asked.

"I love you," he replied.

He gazed into her sultry, green eyes. "You're my wife," he said in awe. A shy smile teased her lips, drawing his attention to her full, sensual mouth. "Enough talk," he said, his tone harsh as he swept her into his arms. Then he lay her down on his pallet beside the warmth of the fire.

The glow of the flames made her black hair gleam and warmed her skin so that it glowed like amber honey. Her eyes and her arms beckoned him. He moved over her, covering her with his warmth. A sigh escaped her lips as he rested all his weight on her. Her arms came around his neck and she kissed him with a tenderness that deepened with every stroke of her tongue until he was reeling with the intoxication and finesse of her lips. She surrounded him with her lavender scent. Her strong hands stroked his skin. His heart pounded in his chest, and his breathing became labored as he tried to kiss and touch every inch of her trembling flesh.

She gasped as his fingers grazed the skin of her stomach and then lower still. Sensation shot through her limbs as his fingers stroked her heat. Soft gasps escaped her lips as an aching need grew and spread throughout her entire body. She arched her back, pressing her hips into his touch. His lips trailed down her throat and then curved around the peaks of her breasts. He slowly caressed each sensitive mound with his tongue. Her hands dug into his long, black hair as she cried out. Searing desire struck her core like fiery streaks of lightning. She begged for more, wanting him to fill her. She needed to be his.

He could hold back no longer. He shifted over her and felt her legs open for him. Then he entered her with one smooth thrust. She cried out, wrapping her legs around him, pressing him deeper and deeper inside of her. She enclosed him within her tight sheath, meeting each of his thrusts with a fervor of her own. Her ragged breaths and urgent groans fed his desire. He lost himself to the ache that erupted within him like a blazing torrent of sensation that rippled through his body. She shuddered around him, her honeyed pleasure coaxing him over the edge. He cried out from the sweet agony that gripped his body and he collapsed, lost in a euphoric haze.

THE SAME BLISSFUL, sultry haze clung to their hearts and bodies as they remained sequestered in their hut for two days and two nights. They left only to see to their most basic needs, but to all else they refused any consideration. They let the world slip beyond their reach, erecting a shield of pleasure and fulfillment to distance themselves from the looming uncertainty.

She could not remember ever being more content. Laughter filled their quarters. He had become everything to her, more profound than she could have ever imagined when, for so long, he had only been a fantasy, something loved at a distance. Their love had blossomed from a wistful flower to something rooted and strong and growing in grace and purpose like the very emblem of their clan: the mighty Scottish pine. For that was what their love was—mighty and grand, something that transcended desire and affection and had become like air to breath and food to nourish. Garik had become essential to her very survival.

His sleeping body curved around hers, and she nestled closer to his warmth. She looked at his strong hand resting possessively on her stomach. Closing her eyes, she breathed in his scent and listened to the sound of his even breaths.

A glimmer of light peeked beneath the door, drawing her gaze. It could not be morning already. Her eyes widened as fear gripped her heart. Slowly, she pulled free from his grasp and tiptoed to the doorway. She eased it open, letting the light fall upon her bare curves. With a sigh she realized it had been the moon she saw, bright and bursting with fullness. The night was still theirs.

She felt the gentle warmth of her plaid as Garik wrapped it about her shoulders. She smiled when his body pressed against hers from behind. "Although 'tis unlikely anyone will be out wandering the village paths at this time of night, I would rather not share the feast of your body with anyone," he said.

"Even the moon?" she purred as she turned in his embrace.

"Even the moon," he said, sweeping her into his arms.

He cherished the feel of her lush curves as he carried her back inside.

"I long to go with ye, ye ken," she said, "to fight by your side."

He stopped and looked down at her. "You say that, but I do not believe you truly understand what longing is. I long for the war to end. I long for days without another's blood clinging to my body. I long to feel the sun on my bare skin, to throw off my armor." He set her on her feet. "Have conviction to fix wrongs, but long only for what your heart desires, what it truly craves. And what your heart craves is this—" He kissed her long and hard. Then he pulled slowly away. "And this." He turned her around so that the bare skin of her back pressed against his chest. His hands curved around each of her breasts. "And this," he whispered.

He loved her that night as if it were to be his last, catapulting her soul to soar as high as the stars in the heavens. He fed her spirit with every tender and ardent stroke of his hand and every touch of his lips to her skin, nourishing her with love so she might sustain her hope during his absence. And in return she gave to him everything she possessed—all her strength, all of her being, all her love to carry with him over the sea and through the lands gripped by war's dark fist. They collapsed in slumber with their souls replete so that when the sun at last rose and bid them open their eyes, they faced the new dawn together.

They stood beside his ship, he absently stroking her hair. "I did not mean to dismiss you last night when you said you wished to fight. You are a woman of passion and courage, of course you wish to fight." He shifted then, seeking her gaze. "But my own courage would fail if ever you took to the battlefield. Forgive me, but I am happy you must remain behind." He pressed a kiss to her lips. "I would have you live," he whispered. "This world is a far better place with you in it."

Chapter Twenty

New Park on the outskirts of Stirling Castle

June 1314

G arik, along with a force of five hundred Highland warriors, held position amid the trees on top of Gillies Hill. Flanked by Logan and Duncan, he stood in the frontline. From the hilltop, he could see New Park, a narrow strip of land, dotted with towering trees and carved in half by a river called the Bannock Burn. Across the Burn, and beyond large patches of murky swamp land, the English army readied for battle. Edward the Second had assembled fifteen thousand foot soldiers and three thousand heavy cavalry at Berwick upon Tweed and marched his army north in an attempt to cease the Scottish siege of Stirling Castle.

Garik looked over his left shoulder at the castle in question. He did not doubt it would be theirs. With an army of only six thousand foot soldiers and no heavy cavalry to speak of, the Bruce's army stood poised to accept Edward's challenge. Garik had been unable to conceive of an army of such size when rumors of its approach first reached Stirling; that is, until the mammoth enemy had arrived. But if the Scottish war for independence had taught Garik anything, it was that size mattered little.

His eyes shifted to their own side of the Burn, drawn by a line of Scottish soldiers riding Galloway nags, which were rugged ponies used for reconnaissance and ambush attacks. Against the English cavalry, who rode large chargers, they would be crushed, and so they moved from the fore to take up position behind the Scottish infantry. Then Garik scanned the men who stood near and a smile curved his lips. The Scottish army had something the English lacked—a Highland infantry.

Garik faced the enemy without fear. Like his king had boasted years ago, their greatest weapon was their superior knowledge of the land—and never had this been truer. Because of the river dividing their armies, the enemy could only deploy as many knights as could cross the bridge at once. To avoid the bridge meant the English would have to attempt the swamps. Given the weight of their warhorses and the armored knights those beasts carried, they would no doubt sink into the muck and likely never clear the river. The only option remaining would be to move farther down the shore to dryer land, but still, they would have to cross the water, and this time without a bridge.

Movement at the base of the hill snagged his attention.

"The king comes this way," he said to Logan.

The Bruce rode a small, brown palfrey with the visor of his helmet drawn, but Garik knew him by the coat of arms on his shield: a yellow background with a blood red cross, at its center a helmet; and above it all a blue lion rampant. The Bruce rode toward them, picking his way around the trees while he made his ascent. Stopping in front of Angus Og, who stood only a few feet away from Garik, he slid from his mount.

"My hope rests in thee," the king said, placing his hand on Angus Og's shoulder. Then with a dip of his head to the rest of Highlanders, the king mounted and returned to New Park where the Scottish infantry moved into position.

Angus Og turned to face his men. "The king places his hope in us," he cried out for all to hear. "We, the men of the Isles, hold the hope of Scotland's king." The hill erupted with the various battle cries of the Highland warriors. The Bruce's words, Angus Og's fury, and the thunderous roars pouring forth from the hearts of the surrounding warriors came together in Garik's mind, filling him with an eagerness for battle. They were on the side of right—this he did not doubt. Regardless of the size of their enemy, they would push the English out of their borders once and for all.

Even if Garik could not have seen the English advance from his position on the hill, he would have heard the clanging of armor and the pounding of their horse's hooves. He gripped his Viking battle ax in one hand and his Highland targ in the other.

"We are ready for them," Angus Og cried. "Let them come."

Amid the throng of Highland warriors Garik was the only one not clad in his clan's plaid. He wore his leather jerkin and a shirt of mail. For armor, many of the other Highlanders wore padded shirts beneath their plaids and leather gauntlets, but like Garik they wore no helmets. There long hair hung in fierce disarray. When ordered, they would rain down upon the English like the savages their enemy made them out to be.

The first sign of their foe breeching the river was the colors Garik recognized as belonging to the Earl of Hereford. His banner boasted blue, gold, and silver stripes with six lions rampant. A call for the Scottish infantry to tighten their formation rent the air.

"They are going to form the Schiltron," Duncan said eagerly.

The Scottish foot soldiers raised their shields into position and clustered together into a tight circle, merging as if into one warrior, and from out of this armored being rose countless long spears, ready to sink into the weak chinks in the approaching knights' armor. Garik watched for which of the Scottish lieutenants would take the lead of their vanguard company. A rider came to the fore and the sight of the commander made Garik's heart soar. It was the Bruce himself.

"Our king leads his men," Angus Og shouted to the warriors behind him. The hill came alive with the energy of the warriors' blood lust.

Garik knew every man on that hill wished to be beside their king, but they would not descend upon the English until Angus Og gave the signal. They were hungry for battle but greater than their lust was their discipline.

Garik watched the English cavalry cross over the bridge and weave through the sparse woods of New Park with their lumbering mounts, the trees forcing them to break formation again and again. The Schiltron advanced toward the enemy undeterred by the trees, which easily passed through as the formation curved around them like a wave hugs the shore. In between the Schiltron's spear men, Garik spied mixed infantry with their knives and axes at the ready to protect the spear men and to finish off the cavalry when they fell.

"Look there," Logan shouted, pointing to a knight who had broken rank and was now charging toward their king.

"Garik, ye ken all of their blasted crests. Who is that?" Duncan growled.

"It is Sir Henry de Bohun. He is the Earl of Hereford's nephew." Garik ceased talking and held his breath. Their king now faced mortal danger. Henry de Bohun thundered across New Park atop his fierce charger. The king, riding his small palfrey, looked like a child in comparison.

"The Bruce is armed only with a battle axe," Garik said as he watched de Bohun lower his lance into position and charge ever faster. Fear for his king gripped Garik's heart, but just as de Bohun was upon him, the Bruce jerked to the side, ducking de Bohun's lance. Then he straightened up in his stirrups and brought his ax down with such strength that he split du Bohun's skull in half, helmet and all. The hillside erupted with roars of triumph as the dead Englishman slid to the ground.

The Earl of Hereford screamed with fury, ordering the men in his command to advance. The Scottish Schiltron held firm. The English cavalry continued their charge. Those not wise enough to pull back before they reached the Schiltron were skewered on the long spears.

"The Schiltron advances," Garik shouted.

"Look at the Earl of Hereford now," Logan said. The Earl, unable to control his troops, retreated. Confusion claimed the English ranks, but then a fresh wave of English cavalry charged from the side where dryer land allowed their horses to pass in greater number. Garik's heart pounded with fury. Then the low croon of a horn filled the air.

Angus Og turned around and shouted. "'Tis the call of our king," he cried.

The battle cry of the MacKinnon tore from Garik's lips as he charged beside his brothers in battle down the wooded hillside. He imagined they were a terrific sight—savage, half naked, and hungry for blood. They thundered toward the confused cavalry with ferocious might and lethal intent. Garik leapt for an English knight, pulling him from his horse. The knight lay pinned to the ground beneath the weight of his armor. Seizing his helmet, Garik sliced the enemy's head from his neck with one swing of his ax. Then he pulled himself onto the horse and charged deeper into the fray.

It felt like mere seconds passed before the English troops began to retreat. As the last of the English cavalry raced back over the Bannock Burn, the Bruce dismounted from his horse to stand before Angus Og and raised his bloody ax high in the air while a cry of triumph tore from his lips. New Park erupted in a chorus of cheers as the Scots celebrated their victory.

While the fire of triumph still burned within their hearts, they turned to the unhappy tasks of attending to the dead and searching for prisoners.

"Send out the Galloway nags. I would know our enemy's plan," the Bruce said to Angus Og.

Garik saw two of their light cavalry head off into the wooded hills, riding rugged ponies that easily navigated the narrow pathways.

A while later the scouts returned and reported that the English had not retreated beyond their camp.

"They mean to try us again in the morn," Lord Douglas said, joining them. Garik greeted the young lieutenant just as two priests passed by, reminding him of the Scottish lives lost despite the ease of their victory. He had already helped dig many of the graves that would cradle the bodies of their fallen brothers. With a silent prayer, he turned back to James who had already begun discussing tomorrow's strategy. Then a thin voice interrupted. Garik turned around and was surprised to find Finn MacLean, Balfour's youngest brother. Like the rest of them, blood splattered his face and plaid, but despite their victory, his shoulders stooped with defeat.

"My lords," he said, kneeling before Angus Og and Lord Douglas.

"My brothers are among the dead," Finn said.

Ronan came forward. "I am sorry for your loss," he said.

"Keep away," Finn snapped at Ronan. "I ken ye do not mourn their passing, but my father will," he said, turning once more to face Angus Og. "With your permission, I will return to Mull and bring my brothers' swords to my father who, God willing, will still be alive to accept them."

Angus Og stood in silence for several moments, but then his hand came down upon Finn's shoulder. "This war has taken enough from the Mull MacLeans. I ken your father is not long for this world. Ye must go and bring comfort to your clan." A tear fell down Finn's cheek as he stared up at Angus Og in bewilderment.

Garik could not help but feel badly for this youngest son of Darach MacLean. He clearly found himself in a position that was not only never planned, but Garik could tell it was unwanted.

"Finnean MacLean, by my trove, I am aggrieved for your loss," Ronan said. "I will call upon ye when we make our return to Mull. I hope we can continue our discussions of peace."

Finn's shoulders stooped further still, but then he closed his eyes and drew a deep breath, appearing to stand a little taller. "That is also my hope," he said.

"We will see that your brothers are buried with every honor," James said, offering Finn his condolences.

"Thank ye, my lord," Finn said. "But I've already seen it done. They were buried alongside their men just as they would have wanted." He turned away then, shuffling under the weight of his dead brothers' swords.

"'Tis a shame for the MacLeans," James said, when Finn was out of ear shot. "Although he is the more decent man, he lacks the strength to lead."

"I would not dismiss Finn altogether," Ronan said. "'Tis a wonder how tall and straight a man can stand when he is no longer trod upon. I wager there is more to Finnean MacLean than meets the eye."

"For the sake of his people, let us hope ye're right," Angus Og said.

"Ye ken this changes everything," Duncan said.

Garik, Logan, Duncan, and Ronan stood in silent reflection, each man knowing the others' thoughts. The loss of both Balfour and Calum brought the promise of change to Mull. A century's long feud may have just come to an end. With the prospect of winning both the war against England and the war at home, the Mull MacKinnon smiled at each other, their hearts brimming with hope for peace.

Chapter Twenty One

The morning sun alighted upon tall grasses that stretched beyond the forest of New Park. The small open plain abutted the Scottish side of the Bannock Burn not surrounded by marshland. Garik stood on the boundary marking where the safe refuge of the wood ended and the open expanse of field began.

The Highland warriors stood beating their shields with the butts of ax and dirk. The sound thundered across the plain, no doubt chilling the hearts of the demoralized English army gathering on the other side of the Burn. At the front of the Scottish defense were four separate Schiltrons, which stood at the ready, each one an armored unit with innumerable, threatening spikes.

James called Garik over. "Gather men and hide amid the Schiltrons. Protect the spear men, and when the opportunity arises, strike down the enemy."

Garik did as he was bid. He dispersed the MacKinnons among the spear men, and then he too hunkered down beneath their shields. Peering through a slit, Garik strained to gauge the enemy's position. Then suddenly a whirring sound filled the air.

"Tighten the shields," Garik heard a voice cry. The shields overlapped, deflecting hundreds of arrows, which rained down upon the spear men. Garik stooped lower, knowing the English archers would once more stretch their longbows to the sky. He raised his own targ while he waited, listening. Then he heard James's command for the Scottish cavalry. Garik dared to spread apart two of the spear men's shields. He peered out just as rugged ponies emerged from the wood and descended upon the unsuspecting archers before they could release another volley.

The English command to advance roared across the plain. The Earl of Gloucester, with his colors of gold and red, led the first charge, but Garik nearly burst out from hiding when he witnessed many of the English infantry hesitate. Fear already claimed their enemy. Blinded by rage, the earl continued his charge, despite the paltry number of men who had actually heeded his order. He advanced toward certain death. With a single word from the Bruce, the Highland infantry raced across the plain. They surrounded the earl and his few followers, killing them all.

Still, another wave of English infantry charged, but the Scottish Schiltrons gave no quarter. The enemy struggled to hold their position, and then their formations scattered. In the distance, Garik could see the English soldiers in the rear already begin to retreat. Victory was theirs.

The Schiltrons broke apart as the Scots raised their spears, swords, and axes to the sky. Odds had been against them, but their smaller army had dominated the battle grounds. They had done the impossible—taken Stirling Castle and driven off the mighty English forces.

Logan and Duncan came running at Garik, relief and wonder colored their exclamations of triumph. Garik's heart raced as he raised his face to the sky. The warmth of the sun caressed his skin and conjured memories of Nellore, but then a movement drew his gaze. The leafy trees near the wood line shook, and a man stumbled out onto the plain. Blood oozed down the side of his face, and he cradled his right arm to his chest. Garik stared, stunned, at the man who they all had believed to be dead.

"Logan," Garik hissed. "Find Ronan. Tell him Balfour lives."

GARIK PEERED OVER RONAN'S shoulder at Balfour who lay on the ground, receiving treatment for his injuries.

"Finn told me Calum had deserted with a band of my men," Balfour spat. "He said our brother planned to break our treaty and attack your lands. So, I went after him with only Finn at my side, not expecting I rode with the true Judas. He led my horse over a ravine. I plummeted down the length of five men. The good Lord alone knows how I survived. Before Finn got to me, he had betrayed Calum, only Calum did not share in my fortune. His body will confirm my story."

"And Finn?" Ronan said.

"He left me for dead," Balfour hissed.

"God's blood," Ronan swore. Then he looked to Angus Og. "Ye ken what this means," he said.

Angus Og nodded, but it was the Bruce who spoke first. "Ronan, you and your men may take your leave." Then he turned to Angus Og. "Send forty of my infantry to Mull under Ronan's command."

Garik's heart lurched. "Finn has more than a full day's start."

Duncan raked his fingers through his hair. "How soon can we make the journey home?" he said.

"Three days' time if we push our horses," Logan replied.

"Mull MacKinnon," Ronan shouted. "To me. We haven't a moment to lose."

Chapter Twenty Two

Garik remained a constant in Nellore's mind. When evening fell and she was alone, she would speak to him, recounting the day's events, sharing bits of village gossip. Her troubles and joys were topics reserved for the evening meal, and at night she lay on her side and pictured him lying opposite her. Her promises of love and longing would penetrate the darkness. She would stare into his wintry eyes and savor the comfort of his unhurried and lilting replies, and it would feel as though he were only a breath away. She knew she was talking to herself and not to him, but without her imaginings, she would lack the courage to face each new day alone.

Days hurt less than nights. Often, she found herself too busy to acknowledge the underlying heartbreak that shadowed her every step. She assisted Hamish with the watch, and now that she resided in the village, she helped Anna and Bridget tend to the sick. She found that she enjoyed making poultices and mixing potions, but most of all she loved attending childbirths. When a newborn filled her mother's arms for the first time, in that moment, everything somehow seemed right in the world, despite the terror and bloodshed that so often defined their lives. She had also listened to her husband's council and taken up furniture making. Garik had been right. She loved working with her hands, and over the months since he had been away, her skills had flourished.

That morning, Nellore had decided to rise early and visit her mother and sister. Much to her delight, as she made her way through the village, she encountered Bridget.

"I need a distraction," Bridget said as they hooked arms. "Long has it been since my husband left my side." Sorrow filled Bridget's silver eyes. "It has been five months. To be honest, I thought these days were behind me—one of the few consolations of old age."

"Are you angry with Ronan for leaving?" Nellore asked.

"Och, nay, sweetling. My Ronan is a warrior. This is the fight he has prayed for decades—the fight that will see a true king of Scotland take our country back. I would not deny him his rightful contribution."

As they ascended the slope toward her family's home, Nellore's spirit began to soar.

"They saw our approach," she said, waving to Brenna and Rose, who had just left their croft and now were trudging up the hill to meet them. Glancing Bridget's way, Nellore saw her lady's eyes crease as a brilliant smile covered her face. Nellore laughed and surged forward, but then the bite of fingers dug into her arm.

"Listen," Bridget hissed. The other women must have noticed the change in Bridget's countenance, for they froze midway up the hill. Nellore's heart pounded as she trained her ear back the way they'd come.

"Run", Nellore yelled as the pounding of horse's hooves filled the air, but not from the direction of Gribun. "MacLeans!"

They fled down the hill. Brenna and Rose raced back toward the hut, but Nellore stopped them. "Nay," she shouted. "To the barn. We need weapons."

Nellore arrived first and flung open the barn door, rushing to where their bows rested in an empty stall. Her own sword was strapped to her back, but she also took up a bow and a quiver of arrows. The other ladies followed her lead. By the time they left the barn, the MacLeans were upon them.

"This way," Nellore shouted as she raced toward a wagon. "Lift with me," she cried. They strained against the weight of the wagon, but it soon toppled onto its side. Then they hastened around and took up their positions behind it.

Five warriors blazed toward the croft with fiery torches in hand.

"Nay," Brenna shouted.

Nellore stood with her bow string already taut against her cheek. She let loose the arrow and it found its mark, felling a large warrior who had just tossed a flaming torch upon the rooftop.

"Take up your weapons," she shouted to the three ladies at her side, who stared in shock at the horror unfolding before them. "Kill them," she screeched at the motionless women. Spurred on by her command, the other women jumped into action.

Nellore let loose another arrow, striking a warrior through the neck. Two dead. Three warriors remained.

"Behind the wagon," one of MacLeans shouted. The warriors raced toward them. Nellore leapt up onto the side of the wagon with her sword drawn. A rider surged toward her with his own blade brandished high. She parried the blow of his sword and whirled around, slicing his belly open. She seized the reins, pushing his dying body to the ground, and then leapt onto the beast in his stead. The horse rose up on its hind legs. She had to fight to keep her seat, but gaining control, she charged toward the men circling back upon the wagon. Arrows, released by the might of her women, flew past her and pierced an enemy chest. He dropped his reins and struggled for breath. Nellore surged forward and swung her sword as she passed. She glanced back to see his head roll across the ground. Then she heard a distant growl. She turned to face the last of the warriors. Her breath hitched when she recognized his scowling face. It was Finnean, the youngest of the MacLeans. She could not contain her surprise. His once weak eyes now glared at her with malicious intent.

"I am coming for ye," he shouted. Then he kicked his horse in the flanks and charged toward her. She turned her horse about and readied her defense. Almost upon her, he dropped his reins and raised his sword with both hands over his head. "Ye're mine," he shouted, but then his eyes flared wide just as the whiz of arrows soared passed Nellore and sank into his flesh. His hands grappled at the shafts protruding from his abdomen before he slunk in his saddle and slid to the ground.

Nellore turned around and her heart filled with pride and wonder. Rose, Brenna, and Bridget stood together on the side of the wagon, their bows still held at the ready. Nellore dropped to the ground and was soon joined by the other women. Together, they made their way to the wheezing man's side.

"To think, I pitied ye," Nellore said. The life drained from the small man. His lank blonde hair fell across eyelids that had closed forever.

They turned away then and surveyed the damage to Brenna's home.

The house and barn still burned. There was naught they could do.

"I'm so sorry, Brenna," Bridget said.

Nellore put her arm around her mother's shoulders. Brenna's deep blue eyes filled with tears as she watched the roof to her home cave in, but then she thrust her shoulders back and grabbed both Nellore and Rose by the hand. "It matters not," she said. "The stone will not burn. 'Tis nothing that can't be rebuilt. What matters is that my lassies are safe," she said.

As they moved away from the fire, the sound of horses on the move once more reached their ears. They climbed the hill, keeping low when they reached the top. Dozens of MacLean warriors raced toward Gribun.

"'Tis a full attack," Nellore cried.

"What should we do?" Rose asked. "We cannot follow. They will reach the village before we do."

"The watch will sound the alarm. Hamish will not make a stand against such a number. He will lead the villagers to the caves," Nellore said.

"What of us? We cannot stay here. There will be no place to hide, and we dare not try to make it to the cliffs if Gribun is overrun," Brenna said.

"Should we take to the wood?" Nellore asked. "We can find shelter and food."

"Nay," Bridget said as she stood. "I will take ye to my home."

"But Bridget, the MacLeans are sure to take Dun Ara Castle. 'Tis only a matter of time," Rose said.

Nellore grinned, knowing of which home Bridget spoke. She looked to her mother. Brenna nodded, for she too knew Bridget's secret. Only Rose appeared lost.

"Come along, Rose," Bridget said. "'Tis time ye knew my real story."

Chapter Twenty Three

The wind barreled over the moors. As they headed west, Nellore made sure to watch for MacLeans giving chase. Her heart feared for her people, but she had faith in the discipline of the watch and in Hamish's judgment. She did not doubt that the exodus of the villagers from Gribun was underway. The caves along Mull's shore would offer her people refuge until their land and homes could be restored.

Nellore peered around her mother to where Bridget and Rose walked together, their heads joined in quiet council. Nellore smiled when she glimpsed Rose's stunned gaze.

"There," Nellore shouted, pointing to the witch's hut in the distance.

"Faster," Brenna urged.

Nellore worried over Bridget keeping such a strenuous pace, but when she glanced at Bridget, she was struck by the change in her lady. She glowed. Her silver eyes shone like polished metal. The lines etched across her face had softened. Suddenly, her stride possessed the strength of youth despite her advanced years.

With radiant confidence, Bridget gripped the handle on her hut's round, over-sized door and said, "'Tis my greatest pleasure to welcome ye to my family's home."

Nellore moved inside and felt her spirit lift. Enclosed within Bridget's hut, they had found a safe haven from all danger. Still, Rose hesitated in the doorway.

Nellore turned to her. "Search your heart, and you will find no fear, only habit."

Rose drew a deep breath and nodded. Then she eased into the small quarters.

"Our safety is assured, for no one else would dare enter here. But I would know what has happened to our clan," Brenna said.

Rose wrapped her arm around her mother. "We dare not risk moving closer to the village," she said.

Nellore stood then. "I will go. I have some skill at moving unseen. I know I can get close enough to judge what has occurred."

"I know a way ye can walk straight into the village without fear," Bridget said.

Nellore joined Brenna and Rose as they stood with expectant eyes trained on their lady.

"How?" Nellore asked.

Shoney moved to a line of pegs and removed a dark, tattered cloak, and then she spun around and presented it to Nellore. "Ye can move unseen concealed beneath the cloak of the Witch of Dervaig."

A smile spread across Nellore's face. "Of course," she said, sweeping her lady into a hug. She pressed a kiss to Bridget's cheek. "Ye're brilliant." Nellore took the cloak and fanned it over her shoulders.

Pulling the hood over her eyes, she laughed, "Do I look as fearsome as ye, Bridget?"

"'Tis a start, lass," Bridget said, "but ye need to feign the witch's hobble. Hunch your back. That's it, love. Now, drag your foot behind ye."

Nellore practiced the witch's gait back and forth in the small hut.

"Do not falter. Do not waiver from this role, and most importantly, do not remove the cloak for any reason," Bridget warned.

Nellore set out across the moors with her back bent and her leg dragging behind her. It was a surreal experience to walk in the footsteps of so many women who had come before Bridget. Never had Bridget's story felt more real. To think that so many years had passed while Bridget would have seen the world only through the folds of the same heavy, ragged cloak. It was a cruel reality Bridget had been forced to face each day.

Nellore whispered a prayer of thanks for the providence that had brought Ronan and Bridget together. Theirs was not an easy union, and Bridget had to sacrifice a great deal for her love: her name, her faith, the memory of her mother. But to hear her speak of the past, she did not dwell on hardship. Instead, Bridget spoke in terms of obstacles and challenges that nurtured her growth and strengthened her and Ronan's love.

Would these wars do the same for Nellore and Garik? Would their devotion to each other withstand the test of time because of the challenges they had faced? She could only hope she would find herself in Bridget's shoes one day—old, surrounded by family, and loved by her husband as fiercely as when they had first met. Perhaps wearing Bridget's cloak was a step in the right direction. She decided when Garik returned home, she would tell him of Bridget's true identity—if he returned.

She silenced those dark thoughts. At that moment, she could not think of herself or Garik. Her sole concern had to be the good of the clan. She dragged her body along, nearing the outskirts of Gribun. All was quiet. She moved through the vacant pathways, careful to never break from her role as the witch. A few homes had been torched, but otherwise there were no signs of struggle. She proceeded into the empty courtyard of Dun Ara Castle and then into the keep. The barren corridors and pathways meant that Hamish had indeed led the people to the caves, but what she did not understand was where were the MacLeans?

She left Gribun and headed down to the port, trudging along the coast. When she reached the caves, she set the cloak aside. Already she could hear the quiet hum of people.

"Nellore!" Hamish exclaimed when she dipped her head into the first cave. "All the Saints be praised. When ye didn't follow, we thought ye were done for."

"Nay," she said, smiling. "I am well."

"Nellore," Anna cried, emerging from the darkness. She threw herself into Nellore's arms. "Where are my mother and Brenna and Rose?"

"They are where no one would dare go," Nellore whispered in her ear. Anna nodded to show she understood the full meaning. Then Nellore asked, "Is anyone hurt?"

"Nay," Hamish said. "They pushed us from the village, but they did not strike. Is Gribun overrun?"

"'Tis abandoned. There's no sign of them. Perhaps they've taken the stores and sheep and gone," Nellore said.

Hamish's brow furrowed as he stood in quiet contemplation for several moments. At last, he spoke, "I dare not risk moving the people until we're certain they've gone. Have ye been to the Ledaig House? 'Tis close to the stores, and the MacLeans do have a great thirst for ale."

Nellore shook her head. "Nay, I did not search the whole of the village."

"What am I saying?" Hamish blurted. "What would your father say, if he knew I sent ye out to spy on your own? He'd have my head. Ye take my place, Nellore. I will go."

"Nay, Hamish, ye must trust me," Nellore said. "No one will see me."

Hamish shook his head. "'Tis too dangerous."

"I've a way to move unseen. Do not look at me as though I'm mad, Hamish. Ye just have to trust me."

Nellore could tell Hamish wanted to refuse permission, but in the end, he nodded. "Promise me ye will not do anything foolish," he said.

"When have I ever been foolish?"

"There was that time when I first met ye when ye took on five MacLeans at once," he said.

Nellore rolled her eyes heavenward. "Hamish, I was twelve," she said before pressing a kiss to his cheek. Then turning to Anna, Nellore pulled her close. "Do not let Hamish watch me leave," she whispered.

When she drew away, Anna nodded. "Be careful, Nellore," she said.

Nellore stepped beyond the cave and said farewell to the bright sunshine before she hid once more beneath the witch's dark cloak. Then she shuffled back to Gribun. This time, however, she headed toward the outskirts on the eastern rim. The moment the Ledaig House came into view, she knew Hamish had been right. Barrels of ale were strewn about the grounds surrounding the long hall, but all was quiet. She peered inside the door. It was filled with MacLean warriors whose mouths gaped open while they slept off the effects of their revelry.

Chapter Twenty Four

Garik plunged his oar deep into the waters of the Sound of Mull. Fiery pain shot through the muscles of his back and shoulders, and still he pushed on, raking his oar through the heavy water. He longed to believe Nellore was alive and well, mayhap training with Hamish or visiting with the clan's lady, but the moment Balfour stumbled out from the woods and confessed his brother's nefarious deeds, he knew his wife was in danger.

"Move, lads," Ronan said as he too strained against the oar. The afternoon sun shined in their eyes, and the wind whipped the water into a frenzy of challenging currents. Garik glanced back. The teeming cliffs of western Mull had come into view. His heart soared at the sight, but then something caught his eye. His mouth fell open. He lunged to his feet, releasing his oar.

"It cannot be," Garik exclaimed. "Smoke rises from the witch's hut."

"What?" Ronan said as he too stood. Duncan and Logan followed behind.

"I cannot believe my eyes," Garik murmured.

"What can this mean, Grandfather?" Logan said. Like Logan, Garik looked to their laird for answers, but Ronan said nothing. He only stared at the gray plume of smoke, his eyes riveted on the fearsome hut.

"'Tis a bad omen," Duncan said.

Ronan moved to the bow of the ship and continued to stare. Then he turned and, with eyes alight with triumph, he cried out. "Nay, this is no omen." Then he turned and pointed to the hut as their ship drew ever closer. "'Tis my love," Ronan said.

Garik raised a questioning brow at Logan, whose only reply was a baffled gaze of his own.

"Pick up your oars," Ronan ordered.

No one moved. They stood and stared, dumbstruck.

Ronan withdrew his sword and charged at Garik. Pushing him against the mast, Ronan pressed his blade along Garik's neck. "Pick up your oars and row or so help me—" he growled.

The other men wasted no time returning to their seats. "Row," Ronan hissed in Garik's face. When Ronan's steel fell away, Garik scrambled to his seat and took up his oar.

"Pull into port there," Ronan commanded.

"Ye want us to make port in the waters of the witch?" Duncan said. "My laird, I've never given much credence to the legend, but then, I've never seen smoke rising from her hut."

"Just do it," Ronan shouted.

Garik hurried to carry out the laird's orders. Everyone moved about the deck, preparing to make port, each man wearing the same bewildered expression.

The shallow draft of their ship allowed them to sail close to shore. Ronan leapt out and began immediately climbing the cliffs toward the surface. Logan turned to Cormac. "I'm going ashore with Garik and Duncan. Ye stay here. Let no man follow. When the ships with the king's men come into view, see that they do not make port."

As Garik pulled himself higher up the cliff side, he clung to his grandfather's assertion that he need not fear the witch. His confidence waned, however, when the round door with the menacing snake came into view.

"Ronan," Duncan called after his laird. "This is madness."

Ronan stormed toward the hut, but then he froze. Garik followed his gaze out over the moors. A figure approached wearing a long, tattered cloak and walking with a pronounced shuffle.

"For the love of God," Duncan cursed. "Everyone, back to the ship."

Garik turned to flee but stopped when he saw Ronan race toward the figure.

"Shoney," Ronan yelled.

"Grandfather, nay," Logan shouted.

"Shoney," Ronan cried again.

"Who is Shoney?" Duncan said.

Garik shook his head and watched Ronan run down the slope and stop in front of the witch. His breath caught in his throat as arms shot out from beneath the black cloak and began to pull the billowing hood back. Garik readied his courage to face the hideous deformities of the ancient, three-hundred-year-old crone, but instead he glimpsed familiar soft waves of flowing black hair and bright green eyes.

"Nellore?" Garik gasped as he stood stunned. Then he shook his mind clear and raced toward his wife. She had seen him. "Garik," she cried, but then Ronan grabbed hold of her shoulders. "Where is Shoney?" he said, his voice desperate. "Where is she?"

"I am here, my love."

Garik had just reached out to pull Nellore from Ronan's grasp when he heard his lady's voice. He whirled around and there, in the open doorway of the Witch of Dervaig, stood Bridget, Brenna, and Rose.

Ronan turned away from Nellore and rushed to Bridget, sweeping her into his arms. "My love," he said. "I feared the worst."

"Ye've naught to fear, dear heart," Bridget said, wrapping her frail arms around his neck.

Garik stood with his mouth agape, but then his eyes met Nellore's and he pulled her close, crushing her against him. "I do not understand anything that has happened this day, my love, but I care not. You are alive. That is all that matters."

When greetings were over and the men were assured of the women's safety, Bridget confessed her tale.

"My lady," Garik said. "Is there any way my grandfather, Aidan, knew your secret?"

Ronan and Bridget both exchanged smiles before Bridget answered, "Aye, Garik, Aidan knew."

Garik smiled. "That explains a lot," he said.

"But why have ye kept this secret for so long?" Duncan asked.

Bridget turned on him. "I saw your fear, Duncan, when ye surfaced near my hut, and ye cannot deny Nellore was a chilling sight in my old cloak."

"She's right, ye know," Logan said. "We just faced an army three times our size without fear, but one glimpse of ye beneath that cloak, Nellore, and we were all ready to turn tail back to the ship."

Bridget reached up to stroke Ronan's cheek and in a quiet voice she said, "Ronan risked everything he held dear to bring me into the clan. We had to lie. Your people never would have accepted me."

"But what about now, Shoney?" Duncan said softly, drawing her gaze. Nellore's eyes widened in surprise to hear Bridget's real name on her father's lips.

Nellore stepped forward. "I've told her that times have changed," she said eagerly. "Long has it been since the witch truly roamed these hills. The people do not fear her in the same way."

Shoney raised a skeptical brow. "The bravest of our men almost flung themselves over the cliffs rather than face the witch."

Logan laughed out loud and then pressed a kiss to his grandmother's cheek. "Ye greatly exaggerate," he said.

"Do I?" she said sternly, but then she kissed Logan in return.

"That was different," Nellore said. "They were out of their minds with worry to begin with, and then they saw me shuffling like a madwoman toward them. Who wouldn't be afraid? But the rest of the clan was not here. No one else has seen the witch for decades. Ye've become nothing more than a legend, Shoney," she said.

Then an idea occurred to Nellore and she raced inside, grabbing a burning cinder from the fire. She hurried back to her family and took hold of the cloak where it lay in the heather. She held a flame close to the folds. "This can all end here," she said. "Release the spirit of the cloak back to the hearts of your descendants, Shoney."

Shoney's eyes widened with surprise. She stepped toward Nellore. Her creased fingers stroked the tattered folds. Then she took hold of the flame. A sob tore from her throat as she touched the burning cinder to the cloak of the Witch of Dervaig. In moments, the dark fabric was engulfed. The flames danced. The smoke curved in a sensual ascent toward the heavens.

"'Tis done," Shoney said, wiping at the tears that continued to fall.

Ronan moved in front of his wife. "But will the clan embrace her as ye have?" Ronan said.

"Anyone who does not will have to challenge me," Logan said.

"And me," Garik said, stepping forward.

Nellore plunged her blade into the earth at Ronan's feet. "And me," she vowed.

Shoney closed her eyes and appeared lost in deep contemplation, but then suddenly her eyes flew open. "What are we doing? The concern over my name is a frivolity we can hardly afford at the moment. Right now, there is work to be done."

Nellore nodded. "Ye're right, Shoney. This matter will have to wait," she said before turning to Ronan to give her report. "Your people are safe. No one was harmed. Hamish was able to lead everyone to the caves, and Anna is by his side, helping to keep the people calm."

"Then the MacLean holds Dun Ara Castle," Ronan gritted.

"Nay," Nellore said. "They are right now as we speak held up in the Ledaig House. They must have been drawn to the stores there, for they appear to have done naught but celebrate their victory. When I spied them not two hours ago the few who did not appear to be in a stupor were pouring enough ale down their throats to invite oblivion."

"I will call for the rest of the men," Garik said before turning toward the cliffs.

"Let us show the MacLean what happens when they break their word," Ronan growled.

Chapter Twenty Five

The Mull MacKinnon, accompanied by forty of the Bruce's men, marched toward the Ledaig House.

"It is so quiet," Garik said. "Are you certain they are still inside?"

Nellore nodded. "I am telling ye, these men were in no condition to ride out of Gribun. I doubt they could've found their own arses." She shook her head in disgust. "Look at all the empty barrels of ale."

Ronan drew his sword and stood before the door, flanked by Duncan and Logan. Pulling the door open a crack, Ronan peered inside. Then he softly closed it.

"They're asleep," Ronan said, rejoining the group.

Nellore looked about. Everyone's face wore the same puzzled expression. "What's to be done?" Garik said, breaking the silence.

Logan stepped forward. "Let us wake them and end this feud right here, right now," he said. "We will teach them a lesson they will not soon forget."

"Nay," Nellore said. "Ye cannot attack men incapable of drawing their own swords."

"The folly is theirs, Nellore," Duncan said, "Logan is right. We can end this feud here. We can silence the MacLean forever."

"Nay, Ronan, listen to me," Nellore pleaded. "These men are not fit for battle. To attack will only increase the hatred between our clans. May I remind ye," she said, eyeing Logan and Duncan, "that our people wait in the caves, scared but unharmed. We've already killed the brother who led the attack."

"Finnean is dead?" Ronan said. "Ye did not tell me this."

"Aye, he attacked our hut," Brenna said, stepping forward. "Burnt it out."

Duncan snarled, withdrawing his sword. Then he stormed toward the door.

"Nay, Da," Nellore said, grabbing his arm. "If we kill these men in this way, then the MacLeans are sure to retaliate. But they will not be after our land or stores. They will come for blood."

Ronan paced back and forth, his plaid swinging at his knees. Then he stopped and reached for Nellore. He cupped her cheek in his hand. "What would ye have me do?"

She took a deep breath. She did not have an answer. "I do not ken what to do, only that we need to demonstrate the strength of our position without spilling blood," she said.

"We are going to lose the strength of our position if we don't act soon," Logan exclaimed. Then he turned to face Nellore. "I ken there is no honor here, but what would ye have us do? Wait until they are rested and risk possibly forfeiting the lives of our men. War is an ugly thing, Nellore."

"Which is exactly why I wish it to end," Nellore snapped. She released a rush of air from her lungs. Her eyes grazed over the army made up of her kinsmen and the Bruce's infantry, all standing at the ready with weapons drawn. Despair clawed at her heart. Then she turned and looked at Shoney, and within her lady's silver eyes Nellore found the answer.

"Logan," she said. "Go to the wood and cut a branch of the Scottish pine." Then she called out to all the warriors. "Each of ye, take up the badge of our clan. Fetch a fir branch from the wood and bring it to me." Then she turned to her mother and sister who stood nearby. "Today ye struck the enemy down. Ye're shield maidens of Mull. Take up a branch—we are all MacKinnons," she cried.

Before long Nellore was surrounded by her kin, each holding the emblem of their clan. "Sharpen the end," she ordered.

Garik stood before her, his eyes shining with pride. "For you," he said, handing her a fir branch, the tip as sharp as a spear. She reached for him and pressed a kiss to his lips before she turned away and moved to stand before the Ledaig House.

"This is our land," she said. "The land of the MacKinnon." Then she plunged the branch deep into the earth. She looked to Logan. "Will ye stand with me, brother?" she asked.

He stared at her with uncertain eyes. Then he slowly released a long breath. "Aye, Nellore," he said. "I will stand with ye." Then he too drove his branch into the ground. Duncan and Cormac came forward, and then the other men followed. Soon countless branches of the Scottish pine rose out of the ground, encircling the Ledaig House.

"Will this do?" Ronan said, showing Nellore a massive branch.

Her lips curved with approval. "A badge befitting a chieftain," she said.

Ronan drove the point into the ground in front of the doorway, behind which slept their enemy. Then Nellore watched with surprise as Ronan reached up and laid his own sword across the doorframe. He strode back to her side then, and together they surveyed their wooden army.

"Now what do we do?" Logan asked.

"Now we wait," Nellore said. "And when the MacLeans awaken they will know they were under the knife and yet we showed them mercy."

"What is it ye hope to gain with this display, Nellore?" Duncan asked.

Garik's strong hand came around her waist. She turned and looked up into his crisp blue eyes. "Peace," she said. Garik pulled her close and she breathed in his scent, but the harmony of the moment was cut short as a third army came cresting over the moors.

"Ronan, what is your command?" Duncan asked as he eyed the riders in the distance.

"Do not break from our current formation," he said. "And lower your weapons." Then he turned, shouting the same order for all to hear.

"Grandfather, are ye certain ye do not want our men to prepare for battle?" Logan asked.

Ronan clapped his hand on Logan's shoulder. "I do not know how this day will end, Logan. But I've lived long enough to know that peace cannot be made from war. Hold your position and sheath your sword," he said.

This time without hesitation Logan returned his sword to the scabbard strapped to his back. "Your men, and women," he added, grinning at Nellore, "stand with ye, my laird."

Before long Balfour and the remainder of the Mull MacLean rode into Gribun, coming to a halt in front of Ronan. "Where is my brother?" Balfour said. "Where are my men?"

"I did not know ye followed us," Ronan said.

"I was not going to stay behind and leave the future of my clan in your hands," Balfour snapped. "Now, answer me. Where is my brother?"

Nellore stepped forward. "Your brother is dead," she said. "I killed him but only in defense of my own life and the lives of my mother and sister. He attacked our hut, which lies in isolation east of here. We were alone. Forgive me, but he forced my hand."

"But what of the rest my men?" the MacLean growled, swinging back around to face Ronan. "I've been to my keep. Finn had gathered the remainder of the MacLean warriors. Where are they?" Then he took a step closer to Ronan and snarled, "God save ye if ye claim your hand was forced."

"Our laird has laid down his blade," Garik said, pointing to the weapon gleaming above the door. "If ye wish him to take it up, then by all means ready your men for battle. I for one welcome the chance to tear your army to pieces."

Balfour glowered at Garik, but he turned his horse to face the Ledaig House. Nellore watched as he considered the army of fir branches. He winced as he slid from his horse. With his one good arm, he bent over and picked up a barrel of ale. A curse tore from his lips as he threw the empty barrel aside and stormed to stand before the door.

"MacLeans," he shouted, but no sound emanated from within. Balfour snarled as he strode toward one of his men and grabbed a torch from his hand. He then lit each of the pine branches on fire.

Smoke billowed. The needles crackled and snapped as they burned. Again and again, the MacLean shouted for his men to rise from their drunken slumber.

At last, the door creaked open. A man with groggy eyes peered out. His arms flew in front of his face, shielding himself from the fiery blaze of Ronan's large branch.

"Do ye see, ye spineless coward?" Balfour shouted. The man followed Balfour's gesture toward the MacKinnon warriors. His eyes grew wide, and he rushed back inside, returning a moment later with sword in hand. He surged forward, but Balfour stopped his charge, bringing his own blade to the man's throat.

"Fool," he spat. "Ye were at the mercy of these men, and they spared ye." Balfour spun the man around and gave him a sharp kick to his rear. "Get the other men up," he shouted. "Ye can walk home. There will be a high penance to pay for your deeds."

A string of curses passed Balfour's lips before he turned back and stood before Ronan. Several tense moments passed while the two leaders locked eyes, and then Nellore's breath caught in her throat as she watched Balfour slowly drop to one knee.

"Ye've won the peace ye sought," he said. "My clan will be held accountable for damages to your village and for any stores they drained. As for your people, there is little by way of comfort I can bring ye or the families of any who were injured or killed. I can only—"

Ronan put his hand on Balfour's shoulder. "Rise, Balfour MacLean. No grave wrong has been done. There are none injured and none dead. There is no wrong that cannot easily be made right."

Balfour stood then and eyed Ronan. "Are we to be allies?" he asked.

Ronan smiled. "It would appear so. I believe a century of fighting is long enough."

WHEN THE LAST OF THE MacLeans dragged their drunken bodies out of view, Ronan turned to Nellore and grazed the back of his fingers down her cheek. "The night Shoney found ye on the moors was a blessed night indeed," he whispered. She threw her arms around her laird's neck.

"Thank ye," he said. "Ye've made the impossible happen." Then he drew back and pressed a kiss to Nellore's forehead. She started to turn away, but then she spied Shoney from the corner of her eye. Drawing her lady to her side, she whispered once more in her laird's ear, "What if there was no such thing as impossible?"

Shoney could not have heard what Nellore said, but she looked at her husband with knowing eyes. Ronan shook his head, wrapping his lady in his arms. "I will not risk her safety or our happiness," he said. A wistful fire filled Shoney's silver eyes as she tilted her head to see her husband's face. "Nellore is right, Ronan. The time has come."

Chapter Twenty Six

Nellore sat in the great hall of Dun Ara Castle with Garik at her side. The tables had been removed and benches brought in to accommodate the villagers, and still the walls were lined with people eager to know why they had been summoned. The gathering rivaled that of the twelfth night of Yule. Everyone had come at their laird's bidding. Shoney stood beside Ronan at the high dais. Even as an older woman, she had always exuded power despite her diminutive stature, and yet a cold chill clenched Nellore's heart as she gazed upon her lady. Shoney's wary eyes darted about the room, and her hand clenched Anna's as if holding on for dear life.

Anna stood proudly at her mother's side, her silver eyes ablaze with defiance while she too scanned the crowd. Nellore knew Anna was ready to challenge anyone who might speak ill of her mother. Beside Anna stood her sisters, Fiona and Isobel. Their stances were equally resolute, leading Nellore to assume they had at last learned their mother's secret.

Shoney visibly shuddered, causing Nellore's heart to race faster. The weight of what she had put into motion settled on her shoulders like an iron yoke. What if she were wrong? What if she had overestimated the capacity of her clan to open their minds and hearts to the truth? What if Shoney were persecuted?

"I have called this gathering to share with my clan a secret I've long protected," Ronan began. "Your lady, who you know as Bridget—a healer who came to us from Skye—has never before set foot away from our shores. Like most of ye, she was born on this island," he said, turning to look at Shoney, whose eyes glistened with tears. His voice softened as he continued. "In fact, her family lived here long before the MacKinnons came to Mull."

Ronan's words honored Shoney's ancestors and evoked a change in her demeanor. She stood straighter. Courage imbued her stance and penetrated her sterling eyes, which gleamed now with silver fire amid her tears. She nodded to Ronan, encouraging him to continue.

"She is Shoney, my beloved wife and your faithful lady," Ronan said, turning back to face his people. "'Twas I who deceived ye all these years, and I alone. I was not willing to choose between my loyalty and duty to my clan and the woman I loved."

He lifted Shoney's hand to his lips. Even from across the hall, Nellore could see the love pour forth from Ronan's gaze as he looked into Shoney's eyes. Surrounded by her family who loved her, Shoney's strength grew and grew. With the hint of a smile curving her lips, she thrust her shoulders back.

"Her name is Shoney," Ronan said again, louder so that all might hear. "She is the daughter of Brethia, descendent of Oengus, King of the Picts. Her family—her mother and mother's mother going back centuries—have lived among us all this while, but they did so with fear in their hearts. Long ago, the women of Shoney's descent faced persecution at the hands of our kinfolk. To stave off prejudice they hid their identities behind a simple disguise. From out of their ingenuity sprang forth a legend of our own making, the legend of the Witch of Dervaig."

When the name left Ronan's lips, Shoney faltered. Silence resounded throughout the hall.

"There has never been a witch," Ronan said, his voicing growing in conviction. "Only Shoney. My Shoney," he said softly. Then he continued but his vehemence echoed throughout the hall. "If there are to be consequences, then I will accept any penalty from the clan. 'Twas I who forced the lie from her lips. If the full truth be known, Shoney wanted to tell ye her true identity from the very beginning."

Ronan's confession stirred a restlessness among the people, yet they continued to keep their own council.

Nellore moved to stand, to speak out, but Garik stopped her. "Give the people a chance," he whispered. Then out of the corner of Nellore's eye, she saw someone begin to walk through the crowd. It was Mary.

Mary stood before the clan but did not speak. Then a smile curved her lips and with a hand on her hip she said, "I've a frightful time keeping my children away from that old hut anyway."

A burst of nervous laughter escaped Nellore's lips. Of course Mary would begin with humor. There were a few other uneasy chuckles, but they tapered off and silence once more settled over the gathering.

"Saints above, what is wrong with the lot of ye?" Mary shouted as she glowered at the crowd. "Two summers past, my Gordon could hardly move, his bowels pained him so. He could neither eat nor drink without his body seizing with pain.

He couldn't lift the plow. I would have lost him were it not for our lady. Because of her healing skills, he is himself again."

Mary's voice became louder, passion filling each word. "She did more than heal his body. She came to my home to see after his comfort, to make sure I was holding up, and to see that my children were fed."

Then Mary turned and faced Shoney. "I care not what name ye go by. Ye've been my savior and friend, my comfort and joy. Ye're the lady of this clan, and there is naught that could ever change that."

Shoney's face crumpled with tears. Emboldened by Shoney's response, Mary turned about and stormed toward the villagers. "She is our lady," Mary cried out. "The same woman who has treated our wounds, healed our illnesses, celebrated our triumphs, and consoled our broken hearts."

Nellore stood then, overwhelmed with emotion, and joined Mary. "Who here does not owe our lady their life or their son's or daughter's life?" Nellore said. "Who here has not sought our lady's comfort or advice?" Nellore whirled around then and looked Shoney square in the eye. "If our acceptance has a price, then surely Shoney has paid in full."

Whispers hummed throughout the hall. Nellore turned on her heel and joined Mary in scanning the gathering with expectant eyes. At last, a cottar, who also lived in the valley, stood.

"I've always longed to fish those waters off the Western cliffs. I'd be willing to wager they are teeming with fish. If there is no witch, then what's stopping us?" he said to the clan. Then he turned his eyes to Shoney, and his voice cracked with emotion when he spoke, "I will never forget how ye saved my leg when the plow ran it over. I was just a lad," he said, turning once more to address the clan. "I owe our lady my life." He whirled around then and stormed toward the high dais. Kneeling before Shoney he said, "I owe ye my life."

He looked behind him at the people who still clung to fear and doubt. "What are ye waiting for," he shouted. "Stand ye fools and show our lady the respect she deserves."

Garik rose and then Cormac and Hamish. In the next moment, every MacKinnon warrior was marching toward the dais. Then, together, they knelt, and with heads bowed they pledged their love and devotion to their lady. Shoney's hands rushed to cover her face as a sob tore from her lips. Ronan pulled his wife close to his heart while tears ran freely down his creased face.

One by one, the villagers fell in line behind the warriors, each member of the clan proudly swearing fealty to their lady. Shoney's hands fell away from her eyes, revealing her tear-stained cheeks. "Thank ye," she said with her hand on her heart. "I fear my heart will burst," she said, smiling through her tears.

Then she stepped down from the dais and reached her hand to Gordon whose turn it was to kneel and pledge his oath of loyalty. She bid him stand.

"My lady," he said to her. Fresh tears fell from her shimmering gaze. She wrapped frail arms around his waist, pressing her face into his chest. Nellore watched as Shoney moved her way through the room, hugging her family to her heart, crying tears of hard-won joy. Before long, Shoney's tears had stopped while she enjoyed the laughter and love pouring forth from her clan. The spirit of the occasion shifted from one of solemnity to that of great celebration. Pipers played, and the ale flowed freely. But when Shoney at last stood before Nellore, fresh tears flooded her silver eyes. She pulled Nellore into a tight embrace. "I am my mother's daughter again," she whispered.

"Shoney, daughter of Brethia," Nellore said. "From this day on, your mother will be remembered."

"Oh, my sweet lass," Shoney cried. "I knew the night that I found ye out there on the moors that ye would change my life. My vision has been fulfilled, Nellore. Ye've brought peace to our land, peace to my heart, and peace to my mother's rest."

Chapter Twenty Seven

Nellore stood beside Garik looking out over the Western cliffs of Mull. Fishing vessels rocked to the rhythm of the waves.

"Nellore," a voice called. She turned to see Hamish holding up a basket of fish before he opened the round door of the hut, formerly belonging to the Witch of Dervaig. Ronan and Shoney had decided the hut should be used as a rest stop for the weary fishermen who were excited by the prospect of discovering the untried waters of Mull. Many had come to witness the new activity.

"What's next?" Nellore said as she wrapped her arms around Garik's waist and shifted her gaze back out to sea.

Garik threw his head back with laughter. "Is singlehandedly bringing peace to your clan not enough?" he asked. "I would have thought you might long for a good rest."

"Actually, I wish to journey to the Orkney Islands," she said.

His eyes widened in surprise before he raised a skeptical brow. "Nellore, you've never set foot from these shores. Are you certain you wish to journey as far away as my home?"

She nodded. "I've never been more certain. Ye're my husband. I want to know ye as ye know me. I want to meet your family, learn your language, see your favorite haunts when ye were a lad."

"Saints above," he said. "I would love nothing more. Only..."

"What?" she said.

"Here I thought I was done asking your father for favors. Now I must ask if I can take ye away beyond the very boundaries of Scotland."

She smiled up at him ruefully. "The Speiring night is over," she said. "I am your wife. Ye no longer have to ask my father permission for anything. I belong to ye."

He smiled down at her. "Nay," he said, pulling her close. "We belong to each other."

"How soon do we leave?" she said, her green eyes dancing with excitement.

"If you truly wish to leave Mull, we will have to strike out before the end of summer to ensure we reach the Orkney Islands before winter."

Movement caught her eye. Nellore glanced over her shoulder and saw her parents, Shoney, and Ronan approach.

"Wheest," she said. "My parents are coming."

"We will have to tell them at some point," he said with a chuckle.

"I ken," she whispered. "'Tis just they look so happy. Wheest, they are upon us."

"Beautiful evening," Garik said when joined by Brenna, Duncan, Shoney, and Ronan

"Beautiful indeed," Shoney replied. "'Tis the kind of evening that can stir dreams of journeying to faraway places," she said, winking at Nellore.

Nellore gazed into her lady's knowing silver eyes and smiled. Then she peered past Garik at her parents. "Where is Rose?" she asked.

Duncan smirked and jerked his head, motioning behind them. Nellore turned and there was Rose and, standing only a few feet away was Logan, both looking everywhere except at each other.

"Och, ye two," Nellore said. "Just go on then and kiss each other."

Rose blushed crimson. Logan cursed, but then with a sharp intake of breath he turned and crushed Rose against his chest. Rose's arms came around his neck. They stared at each other but only for a moment, and then both surged forward. They kissed with wild abandon as though starved for the other's touch. When at last Logan pulled away, he turned to the couples who had shifted their gazes from the writhing sea to the newly writhing couple.

"Duncan," Logan said breathlessly. "I am marrying your daughter."

"Are ye now?" Duncan answered with a wide grin on his face.

"Aye," Logan said, pulling Rose away. "Tomorrow," he called back.

Nellore threw her head back with laughter. "I believe we may have set a new precedent," she said to Garik. "Soon everyone will be marrying without first posting the banns."

"When you know what you want, why wait?" Garik said, his voice deep and unhurried.

"I am looking at what I want," Nellore said, staring into her husband's wintry gaze. He pulled her close and pressed a kiss to her lips. Then they turned back, joining Shoney and Ronan and Brenna and Duncan, and together they watched the sun set over the Isle of Mull.

The End

Thank you for reading The Isle of Mull Series!

May you always feel the pulse of the Highlands in your heart.

Hugs,

Lily Baldwin

THE REBEL HEARTS SERIES

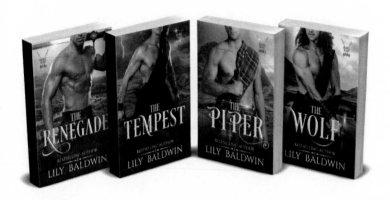

THE RENEGADE

Here's what people are saying about *The Renegade*...

"One of the best books of the year..."

"Lily Baldwin books are filled with tension and desire. One of my favorite authors."

"I would really like to give this story a 10 instead a 5!!"

"Wow!! What a book. Very nicely written, strong characters & love. What more can you ask for. I can't wait for the next one.."

An excerpt from *The Renegade*...

RIFE WITH DANGER AND wicked salaciousness, Lady Elora Brodie had never walked the narrow roads and alleyways of Edinburgh's shipyards, nor had she ever imagined she would, especially after nightfall.

"My lady, forgive me but I fear for yer safety," the head of her guard said in a low voice at her side. "Do not think yer title will save ye here."

"Declan, no one knows who I am, nor will they, allowing ye stop calling me my lady," she hissed in reply.

"'Tis not too late to turn back."

She stopped in her tracks and looked her loyal warrior straight on. The silver at his temples shone in the lantern light as did the worry in his gaze. "My mind is made up. I will not be persuaded from my chosen course."

Declan's gaze scanned the Heavens. "There's no moon nor any stars to be seen. 'Tis a bad omen."

She cocked a brow at him. "'Tis dry at least, which I believe is a good omen, considering that it has done naught but rain these last two days."

"Or...mayhap 'tis only the calm before the storm."

She took a deep breath to quiet her frustration. "Declan, ye've been more of a da to me than my father ever was in life. I love ye, and I love how much ye care. But I will command ye back to the livery if ye cannot accept why I've come here."

His eyes flashed wide. "Ye wouldn't wander these streets alone, surrounded as we are by thieves and beggars and whores?" His voice had risen to mirror his concern.

"Wheest," she hissed. "Remember, we do not wish to draw attention our way."

She pressed her lavender-scented handkerchief to her nose, trying, with no avail, to mask the pungent scent of low-tide, dead fish, and other odors she dared not consider long enough to identify. Lantern and torch fire illuminated the motley assortment of people milling about near the docks in varying stages of intoxication. Her surroundings were unnerving, to say the least, but her humble clothing bolstered her confidence. She wore an unadorned dark-green tunic and a simple black cloak, both of which she had borrowed from her maid, Mary. Even Elora's waist-length golden curls had been coaxed into two thick plaits down her back rather than the intricate style and veils that she typically wore. More than that, riding for two days in the rain had left her garments splattered with mud, allowing her to hope that she truly did appear as common as any of the women passing by.

"Ye're a handsome one, aren't ye?"

Elora turned to see who spoke. Her eyes widened when she saw a woman with unbound black hair that fell in ragged waves to her waist pursing her brightly painted lips at Declan. "I'll treat ye right," she crooned, fluttering her lashes.

Elora cringed inwardly as she looked at the woman whose bosom was barely covered by the deep cut of her tunic, over which her tattered surcote was cinched tight to accentuate her ample curves.

Well, mayhap, Elora hoped, she didn't look *that* common.

Declan cleared his throat. "Move along," he replied firmly.

With a shrug, the woman sauntered away, continuing her search for a man to fill her bed and subsequently her purse. Despite her easy laughter, Elora could sense the woman's desperation. In fact, everywhere she turned, she glimpsed regret and grief sadly pushing through smiles meant to hide the pain of the downtrodden and broken-hearted.

Pulling her cloak tighter about her shoulders, Elora forced her gaze back to the roadside where she scanned the businesses lining the narrow, muddy streets. There was a sailmaker and a smithy, both boarded up for the night. Farther down, she spied an apothecary, which was also closed, but in front of the locked entry stood a boy with no more than ten and two years. He had tangled dark hair, a dirty face, and was selling hot pig's feet.

"My—," Declan began but corrected himself by calling her by her given name. "Elora, now that ye've seen this place, surely ye wish to leave and find a comfortable inn. On the morrow, we can seek out the guilds and find a merchant or another tradesman."

Squaring her shoulders, she shook her head firmly in reply. She was very aware of the fact that she did not have the captain's approval, only his protection. Her steward also did not support her decision, but it mattered naught. After all, she was lady of Castle Bròn. She made her own choices, which was exactly the intended goal of her current mission—to maintain control of her own life.

Picking her way carefully down the muddy roads, she forced her attention away from the respectable businesses to the taverns and brothels, all of which looked the same to her...raucous dens where only the basest of pleasures could find satisfaction.

"Choose one," she muttered to herself, but she knew why she delayed in making her choice.

She was afraid.

Steeling her shoulders, she tilted her chin. This was not her first taste of fear nor would it be her last. Seizing her courage, she took another deep breath and picked a tavern at random.

"The Ship," she declared, looking pointedly at the drinking house across the way where a wooden sign carved with a square-masted cog hung.

Declan opened his mouth as if to try to persuade her once more from her current course, but then he sighed and shook his head. At length, he said, "As ye wish, my lady."

Forcing one foot in front of the other, she approached the slatted door. Just as she reached for the handle, it flung wide. Stepping back quickly, she barely missed being struck in the face by the wood. Raucous laughter and music filtered out on the heels of an old man with wizened cheeks. He stumbled drunkenly into the night. Teetering to the left, he collided into Elora. She gasped, feeling her feet slide out from under her in the slick mud, but Declan seized her arm to keep her upright.

"Where's my ship?" the man slurred, meeting Elora's gaze. Then a slow smile spread across his face, revealing the few remaining teeth he still possessed. "Ye're a pretty bit of skirt."

"Move along," Declan snapped at the old sailor.

Eyes wide, the old man looked up at Declan and nodded, then stumbled backward. When he had crossed the road, Declan whirled to face her, his face etched with concern. "I beg ye to reconsider yer plan. 'Tis too dangerous!"

"The risk is necessary," she shot back. Then she smoothed her hands down her simple tunic and adjusted her cloak about her shoulders. Certainly, she acknowledged the risks she took. Still, whatever ill she faced in that moment or the days to follow could never compare to the lifetime of unhappiness she was fighting like hell to overcome.

Her plan, although perilous, was simple enough. She needed to hire a man—but not just any man. She had a list of criteria, all of which had to be met.

She needed a man who could be bought, who was not overly concerned with his mortal soul, and who was not without connections. He needn't be a laird or a laird's son, but mayhap a laird's nephew or even an ill-favored cousin. Certainly, such a man may prove difficult to find, but she did not doubt that with persistence and courage, she would complete her mission.

"Trust me, Declan. I know what I'm doing."

She scanned the road ahead and set her gaze on a tavern called, The Devil's Bridge.

Once again, she drew a deep breath, then marched across the road, determined to enter the bawdy establishment regardless of what obstacles she met along the way.

Declan reached the door first. "Please, my lady. Allow me to at least make a quick scan of the room."

Singing, raucous laughter, and raised voices carried outside. She raised her brow at him. "Listen to the din. Ye know very well what it will be like behind that door, and no amount of inspection is going to make ye feel better about me going inside or my purpose for doing so."

Declan's lips pressed together in a grim line. She could almost feel the rebuttals reverberating on the tip of his tongue, but he swallowed his refusals, and instead dipped his head, acknowledging her authority. "Aye, my lady."

Opening the door, he began to step out of the way, but then he stopped and turned on her. His wide shoulders filled the doorway, blocking her entry. Uncharacteristically, he seized her by the arms. "Ye needn't fear Laird Mackintosh's coming. Yer warriors would consider it an honor to die in battle for ye if need be."

She shook her head. "No one is going to die. Now, step aside."

His nostrils flared. She knew it pained Declan, but he did as she bade.

Men crowded around tables, calling out to each other over games of dice. Victors raised their tankards high, sloshing ale on the floor and tabletops while losers cursed and guzzled their cups to soothe the sting of an ill-fated roll. Everywhere, women moved among the tables, serving ale and bowls of pottage, or they perched on men's laps, locked in passionate embraces. Breasts were fondled. Skirts pushed past their knees. Elora gulped. Took another deep breath and squared her shoulders.

It was now or never…

"For the last time, Elora," Declan pleaded in a hushed voice. "A place like this will be crawling with the most disreputable men."

"Good," she said with false confidence as she stepped inside. "Because I am not looking for a reputable man."

Go to http:lilybaldwinromance.com to read

THE RENEGADE.

Made in United States
North Haven, CT
19 June 2023

37982678R00129